change whether

THE
REVOLUTION
WILL
BE
WEIRD

WHETHER CHANGE:
THE REVOLUTION WILL BE WEIRD

Published by Broken Eye Books
www.brokeneyebooks.com

Cover illustration by Marcelo Gallegos
Cover design by Scott Gable (using background vector
created by GarryKillian: www.freepik.com)
Interior design by Scott Gable
Editing by Scott Gable and C. Dombrowski

Tremendous thanks to the support of our Kickstarter and Patreon backers
for making this possible. You're all wonderful!

978-1-940372-62-4 (trade paperback)
978-1-940372-63-1 (hardcover)

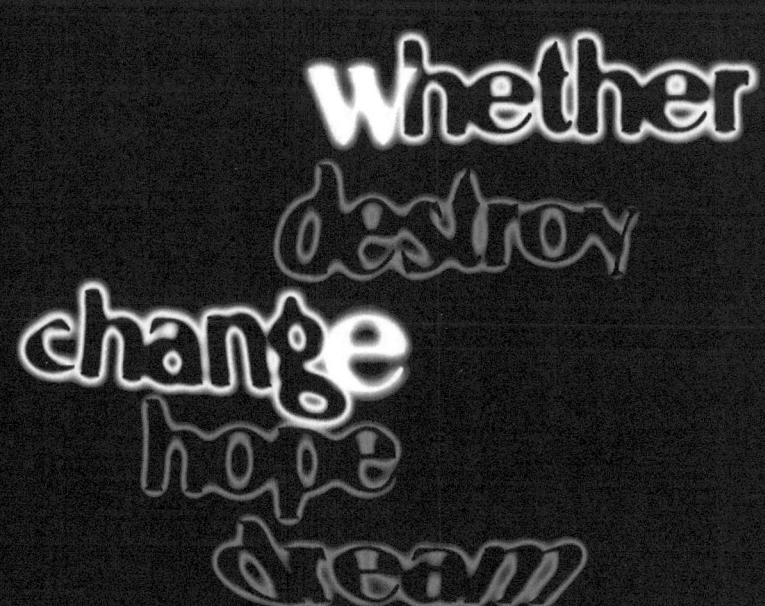

whether
destroy
change
hope
dream

Broken Eye Books is an independent press, here to bring you the odd, strange, and offbeat side of speculative fiction. Our stories tend to blend genres, highlighting the weird and blurring its boundaries with horror, sci-fi, and fantasy.

Support weird. Support indie.

brokeneyebooks.com
twitter.com/brokeneyebooks
facebook.com/brokeneyebooks
instagram.com/brokeneyebooks
patreon.com/brokeneyebooks

whether change

THE REVOLUTION WILL BE WEIRD

edited by scott gable
& c. dombrowski

TABLE OF CONTENTS

INTRODUCTION

Scott Gable

THE YEAR IS _____. OR SOMETHING LIKE THAT.
_{alphanumeric}

And what a fine morning it's been! The _____ haze started
_{organic compound}
burning off, filtering the light just enough for one of those truly
_____ ____ sunrises. It's these liminal moments, between the _____ _____
_{adjective} _{color}   _{adjective} _{noun (state of being)}
that living in perpetual shadow brings and the constant threat of the days without
it, under that brutal sun, _____ your _____, that remind you how
                                   _{transitive verb ending in -ing}   _{part of the body}
_____ the world is. And a(n) _____ sense of humor doesn't hurt.
_{adjective}   _{adjective}

And _____, did we make a haul today! We decided to check out
    _{interjection}
the Ol' _____ land on a whim—_____ and I—the place with
    _{surname}   _{nearest person or pet}
the _____ _____ pits of _____. Those and the giant
   _{adverb}   _{intransitive verb ending in -ing}   _{plural noun or noun (liquid)}
_____ would normally keep anyone away, but we were feeling extra
_{insect, plural}
_____, and it's really the best place for stocking up on _____ and
_{adjective}   _{naturally occurring substance}
_____, so you know. It was certainly a(n) _____ experience. And
_{another naturally occurring substance}   _{adjective}
we won't be doing that again soon.

But it's nearly sundown, so we have to get back to the _____. The always fun
                                                           _{dwelling place}

_____ _____ still patrol regularly, and they will _____ _____ you
_{corporation   compound noun, plural}   _{adverb, intensifier   transitive verb}

on sight, no questions. Who could have guessed that combining _____ and
                                                              _{obsolete technology}

_____ would get us here, huh? Well luckily, they're in détente with the
_{bleeding-edge technology}

the _____ _____. Not sure who to root for in that one, but at least they
   _{alien race   members of a politcal party}

keep each other away from us. For the most part.

   But we're no _____! We've allied with the _____, who know
             _{plural noun, derogatory}   _{monster, plural}

the arcane secrets of _____ the ____. And we've been watching,
                     _{transitive verb ending in -ing}   _{noun}

scavenging, waiting—building our own army of _____-enhanced hybrid _____-
                                            _{technology}   _{animal}

_____ clones. And we're going to _____ _____ the whole
_{notable person (alive or dead)}   _{adverb, intensifier   transitive verb}

_____ thing! Starting at the top with that abomination _____.
_{adjective, intensifier}   _{notable person (alive or dead)}

We'll reenvision, rebuild, rekindle! _____ _____ for everyone! And rest assured,
                                    _{adjective   noun}

no more _____—not worth the hassle. You want a(n) _____ ____? You won't
       _{noun, plural}   _{adjective   noun}

have to wait in line. And _____ ____ for when you're _____ in the
                        _{adjective   noun}   _{intransitive verb ending in -ing}

_____? You bet—!
_{generic location}

   But I'm getting emotional. Forgive me. It's been long ride, and we're all tired.
We're still alive though, finding delight in the world and living for each other. And
you can't silence the spirit.

   You tell 'em we're coming.

Salt Water to Wine

WC Dunlap

The priest sits quietly in the corner of the abandoned basement laundry-room-turned-town hall, watching the residents file in from the upstairs apartments. They move silently as if afraid to breathe, the only sound the subtle shifting of bodies. They enter gradually in groups no larger than three, spaced five minutes apart. The buzz of security drones just beyond the walls reminds them of the risk. It takes an hour for the room to fill.

They carry with them the suffocating stench of chemicals, residue from the war so thoroughly absorbed into their bodies that it now seeps from their pores. It is stifling in this small, crowded space. Trauma can change a person on a molecular level. Chemical warfare does it faster.

A single light bulb hangs from the center of the ceiling. As long shadows are cast dramatically against the walls, the priest is reminded of an old 20th-century painting, *Funeral Procession*.

The people pack every inch of the tight, hot space but give the priest a wide berth. The dusty black cassock and white collar would be a death sentence aboveground. Most avert their eyes. A few of the fearlessly pious nod subtly out of respect but quickly turn their backs. The priest does not mind. This is a moment to bear witness, not to proselytize.

"My granddaughter is Daisy," begins an old woman. "She disappeared three months ago. She is one of many children missing, and the authorities do not care. They told me that there are no resources to search for missing street rats. My Daisy is not a rat. She is a thirteen-year-old child—"

"What does she look like?" interrupts the priest. There are angry shouts from the crowd in response.

"I didn't come here to break the law!"

"This isn't St. Joseph's!"

The old woman hesitates. "We are not religious." She eyes the priest with fear.

"That wasn't the question," comes a shout from the crowd.

The priest turns, and there is Cruz, camo pants and black beret shielding his dark face, a soldier as unmistakable as the priest in white collar.

"The priest is here to help," Cruz continues. "I give you my word."

There are grumbles of protest, but no one openly defies the six-foot-six Black man with two pistols on his hips and a hunting knife strapped to the outside of his left thigh. Cruz has spilt blood to feed and protect this community. If his word is not enough, the consequences of openly challenging him are.

The priest nods in thanks. Expressionless, Cruz folds his arms and stares back at the cleric. After several uncomfortable moments, the priest turns away.

The old woman hesitates before continuing. "Her hair is black, short, and curly, what they used to call an afro. Her skin is dark, darker than mine. She is kind of fat"—there is nervous laughter—"but I don't know how because there is so little food. She has a heart-shaped birthmark on the back of her neck . . ."

The priest begins to sketch. After just thirty minutes, there is a stack of papers, featuring the rough likenesses of nearly a dozen missing children.

"They are stealing our babies!" There is an uproar now. Hearts have been opened, and the anguish can no longer be contained. The community shouts and stomps at no one in particular. Their enemy is everywhere. Cruz and his rebels struggle to maintain control.

"Ooooooohhhhhhhhhhh!" comes a cry from the priest, and the room is shocked into silence. "Father, why have you forsaken us!" The priest stands and holds the stack of drawings in the air. "But we have not been forsaken. My name is Gabriela. You know me. I was born here. This is my community, and you are my people. Whether you are believers or not, I serve you. And God willing, I will find your children."

The screams of the child echo through the sterile halls of the lab. They are inhuman in their ability to pierce the thick walls, disrupting the calm night. They rattle the foundation of the windowless building, barely containing such anguish. Yet the building stands, a lonely sentinel in the middle of a barren field, miles away from civilization—or what's left of it. In the distance though, city lights flicker in response to the suffering girl.

Despite being twenty floors below ground, despite several hundred feet of concrete, her agonies reach the doctor in his study.

A crucifix is shaken from the wall, and Dr. Frederick Linden smirks with satisfaction, a strange reaction to the suffering of a child. He leans back in his leather chair, closes his eyes, and sways to the gentle strings of Bach's *Goldberg Variations*. He can almost hear the pound of hammer, tapping through virgin flesh. The child's wails imbue the lively music with a haunting quality. Beautiful, bewitching chaos. Linden stands, lifts a tattered Bible, weaving it through the air, twirling in triumph.

"Yes, yes!" he shouts, arms stretched to the heavens. "Oh, we move closer to you, dear Lord!" Breathless, he plops down heavily into his chair. "And tomorrow, we bring the priest," he heaves.

Awakened before dawn by a disquieting ululation in the air, like the hysterics of a babe that cannot be soothed, Gabriela gives up on sleep. Restless, she stretches awake and gazes at the sketches of the children, all missing without a trace. And this was but one building on one block. How many others? She ponders her promise the night before and curses her arrogance. She is not a detective. She is but a humble believer in a world that has decided to give up on God. Cruz once told her that her greatest strength was her tenacity for hope.

Lord, let tenacity be a superpower, she whispers to herself.

And then there was Cruz. She could not meet his gaze, but he supported her nonetheless. Beautiful Cruz whom she loved once and betrayed. And now once again, her only lover is God.

But He is not always enough.

She steps out of her gown and gazes upon her body. Round breasts, slim hips, strong legs for running, a belly firm from hunger, an elegant back curved into buttocks made strong from labor. Her body is her temple, a tabernacle of emotion, spirit, and sensuality. It is an altar to which she sacrifices daily, and in that, there is some guilt but no shame.

She runs her hands through short black curls, caressing her scalp, moving slowly to neck and shoulders, across the glorious curves of her form in this daily exaltation that this is she. Far from perfect—too thin, pock-marked and scarred, sunburned and dehydrated—her flesh is more yellow than the deep brown of her youth. But still she gasps in perpetual awe. Her hands move frantically, fearing she may disappear if her existence is not confirmed.

"Hmmm," she moans through full lips that were always too sensual for a boy.

She watches herself love herself, standing before a reflection of a body imperfectly conceived but wondrously made. Hands rub, squeeze, confirm. Breath heavy, stomach clenched, the room fills with her climax.

She needs to begin her day with self-love before she can extend it to others. Light-headed and sated, she slips into her robes and fastens the white collar around her neck. Grasping an old rosary of faded wooden beads, she drops to her knees and asks her God for forgiveness.

Gabriela Ignacia Guerra, ordained twenty years ago by the Society of Jesus as Father Gabriel Jefferson Guttierrez, has begun her day.

Subject 612 shivers on the bare floor of a laboratory prison. They took the blankets because she wouldn't obey, leaving her to lie on the cold concrete, frigid air blowing through the vents. Nothing more than a sheer sheath covers her tiny frame. They murdered her last night. Of this, she is certain. But here she is again—living and breathing, shivering and starving. There is no food this morning, so she must have done something wrong, but she doesn't understand the rules.

The sun is rising. There are no windows, but she feels it all the same. She steels herself for what new horrors the dawn may bring. In her left hand are strands of hair snatched from the head of a tormentor. Under her fingernails is his blood.

The salt of her tears binds them together. Her anger fuels the manifestation. She doesn't realize it yet, but she has begun to conjure.

In a few minutes, Sergeant Ramsey Hale will experience a low-grade fever and the beginning of a rash that will spread from the shallow wounds of a child's scratches.

The sun rises over the gutted remains of New York City. Gunfire pops in the distance, followed by the muted booms of explosives. Almost immediately, security drones are dispatched, darting around abandoned buildings and cardboard-box shelters where residents huddle in respite from the summer heat. Awakened by the buzz of the machines, they pop their heads out of shadowed enclaves and squint into a smog-filled sky.

Sounds of Bad Bunny, Afro B, Buju, Dibango, Flor De Toloache, Cardi, Crimdella, Marley, and the Winans blast from car stereos and vintage boomboxes, setting pace to morning salutations. A conga band sets up on one corner, a human beat box on another, both busking for survival. Old men arrange makeshift tables for games of mancala, dominos, and spades. Parents slather babies with sunscreen, powder, mud, any concoction to protect them from the sun. Couples intertwine for a quickie before it is too hot to fuck.

Children spring up from newspaper pallets on the floor to seek best friends for double dutch, tag, and general mischief. They leap over addicts who nod off in sewage chilled by the shade, needles still sticking from their arms. They bump into sex workers, splashing bucket-water between already sweaty thighs, readying to retire for the day. They shove past poison pushers who offer fleeting moments of pleasure.

All around, there are symptoms of despair but no disdain. Families trade fresh water for boiled eggs, soap for soup, bacon for batteries. Needles are gently pulled from arms, and offers "to watch your kid while you work today" are made. There is starvation and disease but also dancing and laughter. Survival necessitates community, and where there is community, joy is not so easily defeated. The anguish of the night before is not forgotten, only suppressed. Life must go on.

Street vendors brave the heat and push food carts onto sidewalks crowded with sleeping bodies and debris. Some set up shop in abandoned vehicles, preparing to fry meats on car hoods heated by the sun. Their brown skin is caked with thick white screen that does little to protect from the hole in the sky and from that merciless star that brings only cancer and dehydration. In voices heavily accented with the West Indies, Spanglish, and patois, they peddle cloudy water in reused plastic bottles and strange brown meats roasted on skewers and dripping with hot grease.

Many turn away as the priest approaches, lifting their heads to the sky and to the steady swirl of security drones.

"Bless you," Gabriela mutters to their backs.

Still others greet her more warmly, lifting their skewers of strange meat in invitation as she passes.

"Mawnin, Father Gabriela!'"

"Reverend Gabriela!"

"Padre Gabby!"

Gabriela flinches at these well-intentioned greetings. These few have known her since she was a child, and they love her, fundamentalist convictions dying with the old world. But for the old Catholics, she knows that there is uncertainty. *It will take time,* she tells herself and forces a smile.

"Buen día. No hoy, gracias," she answers, denying their solicitations. "But I hope you will come to service today!" she shouts back to a chorus of mumbled expletives and steupses.

She coughs from the thick, polluted air as she walks the twenty blocks to the St. Joseph Ruin. Despite the heat, she covers her nose and mouth with a scarf to filter the air. The dust of war still clogs lungs and rubs throats dry. When necessary, she unravels the scarf to flash her clerical collar to the corner battalion of pimps and pushers. They see the white collar and step aside. As bad as they may be, a practicing cleric is badder.

"You better watch yourself there, ma," says one gesturing toward a hovering drone.

Gabriela spits in the direction of the machine—"I am not afraid of godless men"—and continues on her way to a chorus of applause. She does her best to resist the self-aggrandizement of inevitable martyrdom.

"Subject 612, you did this!" he shouts. "I know you did." He is flanked by another doctor and a guard.

The guard tosses Sergeant Hale's suffering body before the girl. He wears all black in stark contrast to the whiteness of the walls and floor and the doctors' coats. He's heavily armed, blades and pistols hanging from various belts and holsters.

Now the girl knows they're afraid.

She stares back at Linden with wide, innocent eyes.

"Heal him," Linden demands.

They want her to do the impossible, but how could anyone heal the diseased, broken body of the man they dragged before her. Sergeant Hale stinks of shit, and he is covered with sores, pus oozing so thick that it has sealed his mouth and eyes. The girl recoils in horror as she feels the waves of feverish heat rolling off his already decaying body.

She doesn't know how to heal, so she shakes her head, and Linden smacks her across the face so hard that she slides across the floor.

"Dr. Linden, please!" pleads the other doctor. "This type of abuse is not a part of her trials. You jeopardize . . ."

"Don't lecture me," snaps Linden. "I know better than you what's at stake. But I won't have this little witch harming the staff." He turns to the girl again. "Heal him now or no food!"

The girl blinks. She is no stranger to starvation, but the slap has left a deep purple bruise across her brown cheek. She'd rather avoid further pain if she can. Her vision is blurry, and the taste of bile fills her mouth. She isn't fully aware of her actions, but she finds herself staggering across the floor to face the diseased and suffering soldier—Sergeant Hale who hammered nails into her palms and feet last night and hung her from a piece of wood.

The girl looks at Linden.

"Well, go ahead," he urges. "Let me see what you can do."

The girl places her hands on either side of Sergeant Hale's head. Pus oozes between her fingers and drips down her wrists, but still she cradles his head with the tenderness of a mother holding a babe. She gently pulls each eyelid open to reveal cloudy, unfocused whites. Sergeant Hale moans in anguish.

"Shhh," the girl comforts, and with a sudden flick of the wrist, she snaps his neck.

The other doctor screams as Sergeant Hale's lifeless body falls to the floor. A guard kicks the girl in the face.

It was a mercy, she thinks as consciousness slips.

Gabriela takes her time to greet the community and impart as much hope as her station still represents. She stops every few blocks to pass out reproductions of the missing children and to bless the people.

"Have you seen this boy?" she asks.

The people cautiously glance at the drawings but shake their heads.

"Can you hang these up for me?"

A few nod and accept the copies. Others hand her pieces of moldy bread and dried meats.

"Thank you for trying, Reverend," they say.

Gabriela accepts their offerings with a humble, "Bless you," struck by the gravity of their sacrifice. She quickly tucks the food away so as not to tempt the piety of the corner dwellers.

"Why is this happening? Where is God?" they ask her, but she does not know.

"Where there is faith, there is hope," she says to herself as much to the others.

She encourages them to join her for mass, but most shake their heads, requesting a quick blessing instead before darting away, anxious eyes watching the sky for drones. Gabriela complies with a grateful heart for even the tiniest demonstration of faith. She whispers prayers, makes the sign of the cross, and squeezes hands.

Religion outlawed, clerics persecuted, driven underground or worse. This is life in absentia of God.

Gabriela sighs. These people need more than religion from a defrocked priest. They need the living God. Her heart cries for this beloved community of contradiction.

"Belief," Gabriela shouts, "tore this world apart, but it also held it together. They said we were wrong. That we believed in fairies, children's stories to dull the indignities of our oppression. They sought to liberate us from the superstition of primitive man, and they tried to steal our God, leaving us in a squalor far worse than what we'd ever know. But you cannot steal what cannot be contained. Our belief is our hope, and our hope is our liberation!"

Alleluias and *amens* are shouted behind the concealment of bandana-covered mouths, shadowed archways, and fearful hearts. Security drones buzz overhead.

"Aleluya," the girl mumbles in restless sleep. She stirs awake and attempts to rub the sleep from her eyes only to find her tiny wrists shackled to the wall.

"Is that your name?" Linden asks. He sits on a bench against the opposite wall. Two guards stand by the door.

The child jumps. He'd just been sitting there, watching her sleep. She backs as far away as her shackles will allow.

"Is that your name," Linden asks again. "A-LU-O-YE?"

"Nobody is named that," the girl answers.

Linden's laugh is sinister. "I suppose not. But we could call you that."

"I have a name," the child states. "It's . . . it's . . ." She cannot remember, "Subject 612?"

"I think I'll call you Killer."

The girl looks away.

"You killed a man today, Killer." Spittle sprays from clenched jaws as Linden sneers. "You snapped his fucking neck like a twig. How old are you—eight, nine years old?"

"I'm eleven," the child answers, but the doctor does not care.

"I've been doing some thinking," he continues. "I had such high hopes for you and the cultivation of your abilities. But I don't think you're the savior that humanity needs. I don't think you have the compassion necessary to inspire the masses. I think that you're something else. A demon perhaps."

"Your gods are demons," mumbles the child.

"What was that, Killer?"

"You're saying it wrong," the child responds.

Linden raises an eyebrow. "Saying what wrong?"

"It's not Aleluya. It's Yemaya."

"That's not what you said," Linden growls.

"I'm certain it is," answers the child.

Gabriela reaches St. Joseph's drenched in sweat and her own futility. No one has seen the children, and a few more are added to the missing list.

A handful of adults and children await in the vestibule, gather in obeisance to that atavistic fear of a supreme being. They stand in the shade of the ruins, one of the many holy spaces bombed out after the passing of the Eradication of Proselytization Act nearly ten years ago. Three walls, blackened by fire, remain. There is no altar. Pews and pulpit removed by looters, stained-glass windows blown out, the bishop long dead.

Tiny altars to other gods litter the corners of the ruin, every believer wanting to leverage the energy of this once-holy place. White candles surround plates of rat-gnawed dried fish, coconut shavings, and bowls of white roses floating in water. Red and black beads and offerings of cigars and candies and amulets of a single blue eye hang from the walls. Gabriela does not mind. Faith is hope, hope is liberation.

Gabriela looks upon her small band of brave parishioners, defying the law to honor God. She smiles. "Lord be with you."

"And with your spirit," they mutter in response.

There are fewer than yesterday, even fewer than the week before, especially the children, but she is thankful for those who are present. Perhaps she can provide someone with peace today. With a humble and grateful heart, she begins Sunday Mass. "I confess to almighty God and to you, my brothers and sisters, that I have sinned through my own fault . . ."

Stale bread and warm water made holy through transubstantiation are served to souls as hungry for deliverance as their bodies are for food. "Lord, we are not worthy to receive you." They partake with greed in the body and blood of Christ. After services, Gabriela distributes the extra food collected along her walk and apologizes for not having more.

The congregation lingers in the shade of the cathedral ruins. It is just eleven in the morning, but already it's well over ninety degrees, the earth melting as humanity combusts. Few venture outside without sunscreen or wet towels covering their faces. More sit within shadowed corners or nap to wait out the worst of the heat. Even with precautions, faces, arms, and legs are covered with boils and sores that will never heal.

Gabriela grabs a crowbar from the corner and sprints outside to a fire hydrant. She twists and turns with arms too powerful for such a small frame until she is rewarded with a steady, albeit muddied, spray of water. There are children suddenly everywhere and a good share of the old. She rushes back into the shade of the church to watch this rare moment of joy as the neighborhood dances barefoot through the spray, somehow avoiding the broken glass and discarded needles that litter the ground. Dirty faces and tired bodies are washed clean in the cool relief as brown water runs off into gutters. If only she could relieve all pain so easily.

Where is God?

"You're doing good work here," comes a voice from the corner.

"Thank you . . ." Gabriela turns and struggles to remember the name of the parishioner—Romero, Richard, no—Rodney. A neighborhood boy, late teens, emaciated from malnutrition and drugs. He ran with a band of local kids, mostly orphaned. But lately he'd been creeping around the church alone. "Thank you, Rodney."

Rodney smiles at the recognition, scratching the red peeling skin on his face as he approaches the priest. "I was born after the war, so I wasn't raised religious. I don't really understand this Catholic shit—I mean, stuff. But it seems like it's helping. You're a priest, right?" He scans her face and body, questioning.

"You can call me pastor," she answers the unasked question.

"What kind of priest are you again?" Rodney asks. "I mean, there're different kinds, right?"

"Jesuit," Gabriela answers with a tight lip.

"I remember you from before," he continues, but his voice trails off.

Gabriela stares at the playing children. "I've recommitted to my vows. There is no one left to object. I am the church's last soldier in this city. Maybe the world." She laughs to herself at the irony. "Did you know that Jesus died for the lowliest of sinners?" she asks the boy.

Rodney nods. "I guess that's why I'm here."

"Do you need confession?"

"Yeah. I think I do."

There is no longer a confessional in the church, so she leads him deeper into the ruins for privacy, past sleeping parishioners, exhausted from the heat, and addicts who want to feel closer to God. They move into an area where the roof hangs dangerously low, but there is rock to sit on. She gestures for him to take a seat.

"Do you understand confession?" she asks.

Rodney shakes his head. Even in the dim light, she can see the tremble in his hands. His entire body is shaking. Sweat pours down his brow, but it isn't from the heat. She takes his hands into her own. There are track marks on his arms, and his skin is fire to the touch.

"Well, first you must be contrite," Gabriela explains. "You must be truly sorry."

"I am. I am," he answers.

"Then you must confess your sins fully," she continues, "both in kind and in number. Do not withhold any detail, for God knows the whole truth."

Rodney nods in response.

"Lastly—and this is probably the hardest—you must be willing to make amends for your sins. And I will determine your penance. Only through me will you receive absolution. Do you understand?"

"I do," he answers.

"Okay. Now tell me, when did you last confess?"

"Never. I mean, this is my first . . ."

"Okay, okay," Gabriela nods. "Why do you seek forgiveness?"

Rodney bursts into tears. For several minutes, he sobs into snot-and-tear-covered hands. Gabriela waits patiently. "The kids," he sobs, "I hurt the kids."

Gabriela sighs. This would not be the first pedophile confession she's heard, not even the first this week. She suppresses the rising rage and wills empathy for his suffering soul.

"They came while we slept," he tries to explain. "Most of us ran, but I hid and watched. They took dozens. Stunned them and dragged them away. I'm bigger, and I could have protected them, but I hid and froze and watched instead. They had guns."

Gabriela frowns but lets the boy continue.

"They came back, found us wherever we hid, always dragging more of us away. Eventually they brought me food. Told me to tell them where we slept. Before that, sometimes I didn't eat for a week, and they gave me food. So I'd call them on this." He pulls out an antiquated flip phone from his pocket. "Take it. I don't need it no more!"

He tosses the phone to Gabriela. Bewildered, she tucks it into her robe and asks, "Who are they?"

"I don't know. Military-types and whitecoats. They showed up in a van with a snake on it. They seemed official-like, you know?"

"A snake? Are you sure?"

Rodney nods. "Yeah, it was twisted around a triangle, and its head was at the tip."

"That's Basilisk. They're one of the few corporations that protested the Anti-Proselytization Act. The snake is a Garden of Eden reference—'beware of temptation' type of stuff . . ."

Rodney stares back blankly.

"Never mind," Gabriela continues. "They've been using us as lab rats since before the war. We're not their type of Christians."

Rodney shrugs. "Yeah, I might have heard something about them."

"But you called them anyway and helped them take your friends?" Gabriela asks, straining to understand.

"They said they had a mission, that they'd take care of them, so I figured anything had to be better than this place. I asked to go too, but they said I was too old. I thought it was a win-win, you know? They get something, I get something."

"That's not the way our world works, Rodney."

"Then a kid came back," Rodney continues. "Jamal. He got away somehow. He was real fucked up too. He was bleeding and limping, and there were nails sticking out of his hands and feet. I've been coming to mass long enough now to know that they crucified him. They fucking crucified him!"

"What?"

"He found me. Probably by mistake, trying to get back to the crew. He asked me for help, but I didn't know what to do, so I called them. I told him to wait, that I was gonna get some help. They came to get him right away. That was about a month ago. He wasn't moving when they put him in the van."

"You called them," Gabriela repeats in disbelief.

"Yeah," Rodney rambles on, unloading his guilty conscience, unable to stop talking now that he'd started. "I kept calling them too, to let 'em know where to find more kids, because I needed the food . . . and stuff. Even after I knew what they done to Jamal, I kept calling them. Nobody came back, 'cept Jamal that one time. They're all probably dead, right? Does this mean I'm going to hell?"

Gabriela stares at the boy without an ounce of compassion. "Why do you confess all of this now?"

"Because they stopped answering my calls, and I'm fucking starving!" Rodney cries. "They won't pick up the goddamn phone anymore. And I need it. I need it!"

Gabriela stands abruptly and drags Rodney up by the ear.

"Ow, bitch," he spits.

Gabriela shoves him forward. "You come with me now, or I swear I'll show you hell before God gets the chance!"

The girl sits chained to the walls of a white padded cell. Her head throbs from the most recent beating. Her body is covered in bruises. She heals quickly, but it hurts. And she's tired of healing only to be hurt again. This time, there is enough slack in her chains to hold a glass of water. She tilts it with shaking hands to sip through swollen lips. Her tears drip into the glass and mix with the water. She sips that too, but she doesn't drink it all. She wishes she had herb and root the way her mother had taught her. Instead there is just salt, water, and flesh—her flesh—and the doctor's drugs racing through her veins, amplifying instinct, strength, and talent. She is talented. She will work with what she has been given.

Minutes later, a guard dies choking from his own spittle.

Gabriela waits for the drones to pass before descending into the abandoned subway station. She drags Rodney through rusted turnstiles and across pitch-black platforms littered with the remnants of war. They move slowly through the dark, guided by tracks that once connected Manhattan's north and west sides. An abandoned subway car, torn in half, blocks their path, lights oddly flickering. Gabriela pushes the boy through the subway car and makes an abrupt turn into a tunnel leading away from the main tracks. The flickering light of the old car lights their way. Deep within these urban catacombs, there is a nondescript metal door, bolted from the inside.

Gabriela bangs.

And there is nothing.

She bangs again.

"Open the door, Cruz!" she shouts. "I know who's taking the children!"

The door swings open, and she tosses Rodney in first. It takes several seconds after the door has closed for her eyes to adjust to the light. Dozens of men and women in makeshift camouflage, cleaning weapons, counting ammunition, and studying city blueprints. They turn briefly to take in the newcomers before resuming their tasks.

He smells of gunpowder and whiskey, the cocktail for the revolution. He towers over Gabriela and the boy, still sprawled on the floor. Black eyes stare down at her with annoyance and a bit of distrust. "Talk," Cruz orders.

He stands so close that their bodies almost touch. His breath is warm as he chews on his thick bottom lip. He does that when he's nervous. She is making him nervous.

"Basilisk has taken them," Gabriela tries to stay focused. "I knew these kids weren't just vanishing into thin air."

"Basilisk?" Cruz laughs. "The food and drug company? Those theist assholes playing at alchemy while we starve? I'm not interested in your god wars, Gabby. There are bigger battles here."

"Was that you this morning?" Gabriela asks. "I heard the gunfire. The explosions."

"That was just a dry run. We're prepping to take the suburbs. The Walmart."

"No shit!" Rodney exclaims, still sprawled out on the floor.

Gabriela slaps him on the head before turning to Cruz. "It's guarded, Cruz. Heavily. You won't succeed."

"Now you care, Padre?"

"Cruz, I never intentionally hurt you. Don't try to hurt me now."

"I'm sorry," Cruz rubs his head in anguish. "But seeing you in that collar after everything . . ."

Rodney raises an eyebrow.

"This isn't about you and me," Gabriela cuts him off. "You're doing all of this for the community, right?"

Cruz nods. "You know I am."

"Well, there is no community without children. Basilisk has been feeding this community poison for years, even before the war. Now they're taking the children." She kicks Rodney. "Tell him everything."

Four doctors stand before Linden's desk, watching their chief officer wrestle with indecision. He rocks back and forth in his chair, tapping his fingers. He sighs several times, opens his mouth to speak, closes it, and continues rocking. This goes on for several minutes.

"Dr. Linden, sir, we need to know what to do with the child," implores a doctor.

"We can terminate and start over," another doctor suggests. "While her abilities are impressive, she is wild and unpredictable. Like the others, she's not what we intended."

"Wild and unpredictable," Linden repeats. "Isn't that the very nature of God?"

The doctors frown.

"I'm no theist," offers one, "but I recall that God always has a plan."

Linden smiles. "I believe She does."

"Excuse me, sir?" asks one doctor.

Linden stands. "This world needs a cleansing. You are right, wise counselors. These children are not what we intended. But unlike our esteemed Bible-burning government officials, I have not lost the faith. Fortunately for us all, I can pivot," Linden stands and begins pacing the room. He speaks to himself, "I thought I was giving the world the Messiah, but instead I bring apocalypse. 612, I should have known . . ." His voice trails off into thought.

"612? Dr. Linden, sir, what are you talking about?"

"Behold a white horse," Linden recites, "and he that sat on him had a bow, and a crown was given unto him, and he went forth conquering and to conquer." When the doctors don't respond, Linden shakes his head and chuckles. "We really do need to reinstitute Sunday School. Until then, our plans remain the same. We will release the girl this evening. Bring the papist now."

"Basilik is a religious organization," Gabriela explains. She stands in the center of a circle surrounded by Cruz and his soldiers. Rodney sits nearby, his addiction momentarily forgotten. He stares, in awe of the priest. "Their CEO—a Linden something or other—is a devout fundamentalist," Gabriela continues. "Before the war, they printed scripture on every box of their sugar-laden, genetically modified poison masquerading as food. If anyone has an opportunity to breach their walls, it's a priest."

Cruz objects, "They're not just going to let in some rogue street priest from the hood."

Gabriela thinks on that. "So then I'll confess. I'll tell them that I've been leading a small congregation of Catholics, and we need their protection."

"These fundamentalists aren't too fond of Catholics—or Black and brown folk," interjects a soldier. "And no offense, you ain't exactly the typical priest."

Gabriela shrugs. "It's all I got. We worship the same God. That has to count for something."

Cruz nods slowly. "Maybe. But what if you can't convince them to release the children?"

"Then we have no choice. You have fire power?"

The rebels nod.

"Then I'll carry accelerants under my robes. You follow me, and if I cannot convince them, I'll find a way to let you in. Together we'll burn that motherfucker down!"

The room erupts with cheers.

Gabriela leaves Rodney with the rebels and treks back through the blackness of the underground alone to prepare for what may very well be the sacrifice of her life. The darkness and quiet force her to slow as she leans against the subway walls for support. She takes note of the inconspicuous markers left by Cruz's crew to guide her way. Rats scurry on her approach, but she is unbothered. She knows from the meat skewers peddled from push carts that the rats have more to fear from her. She has peace now to quiet her mind, to pray and reflect on the circumstances.

"After this is over, come back to me," Cruz whispered before she left. He laced his fingers between hers. She did not let go. "The movement needs you. I need you."

She laughed. "I think I am better suited for spiritual warfare."

"And how is that going?" he asked.

"Most days I feel like I'm losing," she answered honestly.

"Me too," he replied. "But I promise, we'll bring back those kids."

"I know that we will try." And after far too many times, she let go of his hand again, and it felt like letting go of life.

Lost in thought, she coughs the dust of the underground from her lungs, brushes the dirt from her cassock, and empties each shoe of debris. She doesn't hear the drone until it is inches from her face, its muzzle pointed at her forehead. She backs away slowly, but the drone is locked and follows.

"Remain where you are," a mechanical voice speaks above the whirl of the propellers.

A gunshot sounds, and Gabriela drops to the ground, instinctively lifting her arms around her head. A second later, the drone crashes at her feet, a hole piercing its body. She looks up to a distant roof where a lone gunman waves in her direction.

"We got you, Reverend!" shouts the sniper.

All things considered, she loves this community.

"There's more coming!" shouts another from a nearby roof. "Get moving, Priest!"

Gabriela doesn't waste time. She lifts her cassock to her knees and races toward her home. She takes the long way, dodging through abandoned buildings, zigzagging around people who shout questions as she races from a battalion of drones. Old ladies utter curses and spit their hexes into the air. Old men throw bottles and cans. The young swing bats and pipes at the buzzing machines. Gabriela cuts through basements and into alleyways, maintaining cover from the sky as much as possible. She doesn't stop until she can no longer hear their constant buzzing. She crawls into a dumpster and waits.

The sun has set before Gabriela is brave enough to venture back into the street. The neighborhood awakens from its heat-induced siesta, second morning as it's come to be known. Music is blaring even louder than before, the streets are packed with a bazaar of food carts, soothsayers, merchants, pushers, pimps. She is able to slip through the chaos unseen into her fifth-floor walk-up studio.

The halls are unusually quiet and empty. There are no children running the steps, addicts shooting up in the corners, lovers fighting or making up. As she passes each apartment, many missing doors, she realizes that they are all completely empty. Her heart stops as she reaches her own. Slowly she turns the knob, fearing the worst. As she swings the door open, she is relieved to find that her apartment is undisturbed, exactly the way she left it this morning. But it is time to find a new place to live.

Frantically she stuffs Bible, rosary, and essentials into a cloth bag. She slips on a pair of pants and tosses off her cassock. Rodney's cell phone thumps loudly to the ground.

She freezes.

"Shit."

She'd been tracked.

Gabriela turns to find six red beams pointed at her naked chest. She closes her eyes, crosses herself and prays that the GPS did not penetrate the bunker to locate Cruz.

The van with the snake speeds across bridges, past the gates of strip malls and superstores and the impenetrable walls of suburban homes until there is nothing but yellow grass and black night. Gabriela's captors let her stare out the window into the space and stability that so many are denied. They keep her arms shackled behind her back as a reminder that her freedom will always be limited and determined by their grace.

They approach the solid-white walls of Basilisk headquarters and speed into a hidden entrance that is closed immediately behind them. Gabriela is dragged from the vehicle and held before Dr. Frederick Linden.

The inside of Basilisk is as austere as its exterior. Gleaming white walls and glass offices wrap around an atrium of artificial light. Gabriela looks around and up at an endless tower. Frigid air blows through giant vents, stinging her tender, sunburned skin. There are no windows, no natural light, no connection to life at all. It is a sterile white void. She does not want to die here. She pulls away from the guard whose heavy hands hold her in place.

Linden gestures to the guards. "Unshackle her. She is no threat."

The guards comply, releasing the priest. They step back several paces to allow Linden his stage.

Gabriela finds her faith and holds her head up high. "I acknowledge that I am in violation of the Eradication of Proselytization Act and threaten the state with the theist sedition of worship and ministry. I am prepared to die for my beliefs and for my God."

Linden bursts into laughter. "How long have you been practicing that little speech?"

"But this is Basilisk, no?" Gabriela continues. "We both believe in the one true, living God."

"Something like that," Linden responds.

Gabriela frowns.

"You're not what I expected," the scientist CEO studies her. "A female priest, huh? That boys club at the Vatican can't be too happy about you."

"There is no more Vatican," Gabriela declares, "but I am still a soldier of God."

"And that's what I'm counting on," Linden claps his hands. "Bring up the child," he orders a guard who immediately departs into an elevator.

"Why am I here? Why are you taking our children?"

On cue, videos begin to play on the white walls. Gabriela spins around, confused by the images of children from the city, dressed in their dirty denim rags and cotton tees, herded into crisp white showers where they are stripped and hosed down like cattle. One by one, they are placed in white padded cells. The most violent shackled to the walls. Some cry themselves to sleep. Others shout and claw at the doors. Most resign themselves to their confinement and curl into corners with their backs against the wall.

"What is this?"

The video cuts to children strapped to examination tables and connected to machines. Injections are given, but they remain awake, wide-eyed and terrified. They are poked and prodded, sliced and carved. There is blood and terror. Gabriella tries to look away, but the images are everywhere.

"My God," she exclaims.

"The world is lost," Linden explains. "Our religion bombed, our spirituality disemboweled. Our God silenced by left-wing agendas set on eradicating faith in the name of equality. Yet your people still starve. They still exist in sewage, a life crawling on your bellies like swamp vermin. Turns out, it wasn't God's fault after all!"

"If you cared about my people, you wouldn't be torturing our children," Gabriela spits.

"We need the Messiah!" Linden shouts.

"You cannot create Christ in a laboratory!"

"He only thinks he created me," says the little girl, stepping out of the elevator. She is flanked by two heavily armed guards with twitching fingers.

"Aw, there she is," Linden smiles at the child.

"Oh my God, are you okay?" Gabriela reaches for the child but is held back by the guards.

"I'm fine," the girl calmly replies.

Unperturbed, Linden continues. "Basilisk has always believed in faith-based science, unlike our more fanatical brethren. It's why we're still standing, more powerful than ever despite theist restrictions. We've been experimenting on humanity for years. The war and the chemical mists gave us the boost we needed. These kids, this next generation is special."

"Why don't you experiment on your own children!" Gabriela shouts at the old scientist.

Linden only laughs. "I didn't know that it would actually work. Could you imagine the red tape if we were using white children!"

"You bastard," Gabriela spits.

"Sticks and stones." He shrugs before getting back to the matter at hand. "Now we both know that Jesus performed seven miracles. Well, this young lady can perform two so far. She is incredibly adept at the manipulation of nature—at least water and blood," Linden explains. "And she has raised herself from the dead. Several times in fact."

Gabriela gapes in horror. "You murdered a child."

"She rose from the dead. Twice," Linden repeats. "I mean, even Jesus could only do it once. But before you get too excited," he continues, "she is also very dangerous and capable of committing vicious acts of retaliation. I am afraid that I am not giving you a savior at all. Perhaps that is something only God can do. Instead, I give you Subject 612, better known as Pestilence!"

"You're insane," Gabriela gasps.

"Open the door," Linden orders the guards. "Famine and Death will be ready shortly," he tells Gabriela. "I feel like War may be a bit of overkill, but we'll play that one by ear. So you will come fetch the other children, won't you? I would hate to have to send the drones again."

Gabriela does not answer. She is unable to move. Bewildered, she stands staring at Linden.

The girl brushes past the guards and Linden to take Gabriela's hand. She leads her toward the opening door.

"You will soon be armed with the tools of the apocalypse!" Linden shouts at their backs. "And you will see that what I have done is exactly what humanity needs. A great cleansing. So release these little beasts onto the world and make holy war!"

The girl squeezes Gabriela's shaking hand. "Can you get me to the ocean?" she asks.

Confused, Gabriela shakes her head. "I don't know."

The priest and the child step into the night.

"It's okay," the girl reassures. "We'll all be out soon."

As the door to Basilisk headquarters closes, Linden's body drops to the floor, convulsing and covered in puss-filled boils. The girl doesn't look back, but she knows.

"What are you?" Gabriela asks the child.

"A weapon," the child answers.

"And the other children, the ones that are coming?"

"Your army."

{{
WC Dunlap draws her inspiration from the complexities of a Black Baptist, middle-class upbringing by Southern parents and all that entails for a brown-skin girl growing up in America. Equally enthralled by the divine and the demonic with a professional background in data & tech, she seeks to bend genres with a unique lens on fantasy, fear, and the future.

Sarah Memory: A Fragment of the Revolution

Rachel Pollack

Mother of Silence . . .

Of all the Founders of the Revolution, those who found the Great Stories that make the world, the one whom they themselves revered beyond all others, whom they often described as the "Lover," was a woman who rarely spoke and never told a single Story until just before her death. Many found this hard to understand. Once, a reporter assigned to the "insurrection" asked Jonathan Mask-of-Wisdom about the Founders' devotion to the "Mother of Silence," as some called her. "I don't get it," the reporter said. "It's supposed to be all about stories. She doesn't say anything. She doesn't do anything."

Mask-of-Wisdom said nothing, only reached out his left hand to stroke the reporter's cheek with his fingertips. Blood roared through the reporter's body as if his veins had become out-of-control rivers. He looked down at the ground and saw a vast city under the dirt. Flags and flowers on all the buildings signaled some great celebration. Fierce faces without bodies floated like balloons just under his feet. The reporter screamed and covered his eyes. When he looked again, Mask-of-Wisdom stood smiling at him with such love that the reporter got down clumsily on his knees and hugged the Founder around the waist.

From the first anyone knew of her to her terrible last days, the Mother of Silence lived in a small, stone house on a quiet, wooded road. A simple place, but all the Founders came there, sometimes alone and in disguise but sometimes as a full pilgrimage, all of them, with banners and drums and even fresh tattoos of roadmaps adorning their legs. Their helpers, the ones called Barefoot Workers, expected on each trip that now, this time finally, the Lover would reveal her glory. Now she would tell a Story so wondrous that all the government poison would drop from the air, and the ice caps, which had melted and flowed down in their hunger for stories, would return at last so that the oceans would sink back to their former levels.

But no. She would just sit on her wooden porch, which was always a little shaky, its white paint peeling. And the Founders would sit on the floor or the steps with all the Workers crowded into the house or on the dirt and everyone so quiet they could hear the deer's teeth as they chewed the bushes or the shift of hawks' wings as they rode the columns of air that held the breath of the Founders. Finally, the Lover would smile at them, and the Founders would get up to leave. The Workers would follow, maybe with a glance back at Mother who had begun to water her plants from a bright-yellow watering can. Though the Workers could never understand *what*, they knew that something had happened, for as one of them wrote years later, "Shock and awe filled their faces, and for a half hour or so, their bodies doubled in size, so later we would pick leaves from their cheeks or shoulders and even chase away small birds that had tried to nest in their hair."

How Memory got her name . . .

Even Sarah's name, Memory, did not come to her in the usual way. Modern Tellers all announce their name as a gift from the living world, but the Founders actually brought theirs back from a bleak place known as the Valley of Names. All but this one woman. When so much time had passed that some feared the one they revered as their Mother might actually die nameless, Rebecca Rainbow suggested they simply choose a name for her and trust the Living World to guide them to the right choice. Though everyone liked the name that Rainbow suggested—Sarah Brightnoise—they rebelled at the idea of simply making something up. They decided finally that one of them would make a second trip to the valley and bring back a true name for the Silence. They cast Sticks and Stones, the ancient oracle for anything to do with names, and the choice fell to Mirando Glowwood.

The entrance to the valley lay in a garage on W. 32nd St. in Manhattan behind a rusty red door marked "Staff Only." The garage owner, whose sick daughter had run in the Parade of the Animals, knew that the Founders sometimes used his garage, for he could hear the parked cars growl with excitement, and the headlights would flash on and off all up and down the seven levels. But even he had no idea what lay behind the red door. He'd never dared to open it.

Glowwood drove into the garage disguised as a customer in a silver car. He parked on the lowest level and was only a few feet from the door when Li Ku Unquenchable Fire stepped in front of him. Now, Li Ku was known even then in those first days as the dark pulse in the heart of the Revolution, and even many of the Founders were frightened of her. Glowwood shook his head; unconsciously his hands clenched into fists as if they wanted to rise on their own and beat her implacable face. "No," he said. "They chose *me*. Both the stones and the sticks were very clear." Li Ku said nothing. Glowwood said, "I won't let you take this from me."

Li Ku took off her mask. And then she reached up and removed her face.

Glowwood stared into a swirl of black dust as old as the first stories. He squeezed shut his eyes, and a great rush of wings filled his heart and lungs. When he opened his eyes, he discovered the dust of dead stars all around him and his own face somewhere far away behind teeth as sharp as newborn mountains. He cried out and crouched down with his arms over his head. When he looked up, Li Ku was just stepping through the red door.

Usually, the valley appeared a wide plain under a gray sky, scattered trees between two tall columns of burning ice. In this bleak land, the Founders tracked down their names like a dog in search of food. They would pick up a flicker of movement, a faint whoosh, the slightest scent of perfume, and they would move quickly to grab hold and press the name to their bodies the way someone might embrace a lover returned from the dead. But that day, when Li Ku entered, names rushed up at her in the form of beautiful children, each one begging or demanding that the Founder take them back with her.

Unquenchable Fire paid no attention, only walked through them until she came to an open space. She looked all about until she spotted a scrawny rabbit behind a rock, the remains of a tuft of grass stuck between its teeth. As Li Ku walked toward it, the rabbit bounded off, but the Founder changed to a black dog with a golden ridge down its back and ran after it.

Just before the dog could catch it, the rabbit became a jay and took off into the blank sky, a small twig held in its mouth. Li Ku became a magpie and overtook it, at which the jay dropped to earth and became an eland with long, spiral horns tipped in gold and a palm frond between its teeth. Unquenchable Fire changed to a leopard and chased the eland along a riverbank until finally the eland jumped into the dark, oily water as a rainbow trout, a blue seed pearl in its mouth. A piranha, Li Ku dove after it.

They played this game for seven more rounds until at last the fugitive name stepped into a grove of leafless trees covered in dark moss and became a tall graceful man with thick golden hair, very long fingers loosely holding a gold coin. He looked in fact exactly like a boy Li Ku had loved in high school, before the terrible night she was forced to discover her name and became Unquenchable Fire. "I'm sorry," the beautiful man said. "I'm so sorry. Do you still love me?" He opened his arms, though he did not drop the coin. Sparks like fireflies came off his skin.

Unquenchable Fire stepped forward and looked into his smiling eyes. "You're not him," she said. "You hold a powerful name, but not even you could bring him back." And then she took his face in her hands and kissed him. He tried to pull away or turn his head, but Li Ku wouldn't let him. Tears ran down her face to run in rivulets through the lines and swirls the Visitors had carved into her on the black night of her Awakening.

Finally, she let him go. She stepped back and watched him sway, very frail now, his formerly thick hair so delicate it floated out from his face to radiate into the air. She picked up the coin just as the emptied-out body fell onto a bed of mossy stones. It burned her palm, but she paid no attention.

When Li Ku looked around, she saw a cave blocked by a large stone. She moved the stone aside and stepped through. She was back in the garage.

Glowwood stood with his back against a long white car whose radio sang "I Can't Stop Loving You," a popular song of the time, only later recognized as a message to the Founders from the Living World. Glowwood seemed not to notice the radio. He stood with his hands in his pockets and his head down as he stared at an oil spot on the concrete floor. Later he would claim that the oil had revealed to him his most famous Story, The Woman Who Invaded a Tree, but right then, he only looked angry and defeated.

Li Ku walked over to him and said, "Oh Mirando, you look so sad. Let me give you a gift." She touched the side of his neck, and his head snapped up. And then she smiled at him. A wind rushed into his mouth and down his throat. He couldn't breathe, could hardly stand. His body grew larger, so big he thought he would smash through the concrete ceiling. He could feel great empty spaces inside him and whole worlds between the constellations of his organs.

When Glowwood calmed himself, he saw Li Ku a few feet away with her head tilted to the left and her arms folded. When he looked up to make sure he hadn't broken the ceiling and no cars would tumble down onto him, he heard her laugh, and he jerked his eyes away. He felt like a laboratory animal let loose at the end of an experiment. Only now, he knew the great secret, the name of the Lover. But it seemed so *small*. "Memory?" he said. "That's all? Just . . . Memory?"

Li Ku laughed again, and Glowwood hated himself for cringing. He held steady when she stepped forward and touched his cheek. "Oh, Mirando," she crooned, "you don't understand, do you? Never mind, my darling. Go back and tell them. They will love you for it."

Silence = Life . . .

So that is how Sarah Memory got her name. But if anyone waited for it to spark her voice, they soon had to surrender their hopes. The newly named Lover remained as quiet as her flowers, as uninvolved as her yellow watering can.

For a long time, the government paid little attention to her, for what kind of rebellion could a mute woman raise against them with all their power to control the words and images that filled people's brains from the web and television satellites? Better, they thought, to concentrate on what they considered the terrorist storytellers with their ability to induce mass psychosis. Government "news" reports warned of "weapons of mind destruction," supposed chemicals sprayed into the air by the Barefoot Workers, though no traces of such chemicals were ever found.

Over time however, as more and more of their spy devices fed back the terms *Mother of Silence* and *Sarah Memory*, they understood that, even though they could not comprehend why the enemy cared so much about this woman, she somehow meant a great deal to them. At first, they tried to discredit Memory with television "specials" that pretended to expose the "mysterious figure who has become a silent symbol of a generation sadly deluded into madness and violence." The reporters found teachers (most of whom had never even met

Sarah, let alone had her in a class) to testify of laziness, cheating, violence, and even sexual perversion that young Sarah had exhibited as a child.

As with so much of the government's desperate slanders, in response, the Army of the Saints turned hatred into love. Genuine witnesses told how they'd known Memory as a child, had wondered about the increasing silence that had caused her to fail tests and be held prisoner after school by vindictive teachers enraged at her "impertinence." The answer came to them in dreams, they said. They learned how Sarah did not really wish to ignore the exams and quizzes, but right in the middle of the classroom, the Ladder of Worlds would appear to her, and what could she do but climb? She would go to the very top where no one had ever reached before, and there in the uppermost circle of the uppermost world, she found the *Book of Stories* whose pages are alive with voices that unceasingly pour out their mysteries of mysteries. Sarah, the witnesses explained, did not keep silent on a whim but only so she could hear all the stories. "She's there right now," one of them said, "listening, listening."

And they suggested that maybe her name had come to her because, of all the saints (as they called the Founders in those early days), only Sarah Memory had heard and remembered all the stories. And more, they wondered if just possibly Sarah had absorbed every one of those stories into her own body, which is to say true memory rather than the mental chatter most people mistake for remembrance. No wonder she didn't speak, they said, for every cell in her body was telling stories, more and more of them all the time, and her vocal cords would only interfere. The saints could hear it (so the theory went), could hear the stories in the silence. But even the saints could not listen to all of it; each one could only hear what they could acknowledge.

The government understood nothing of this, only that their "dogs of slander" had failed to turn people against Silent Sarah, had in fact only increased her notoriety. And so it struck someone (later, people would say it was the Torturer himself who had inserted this idea into their minds like a puff of smoke blown into their mouths) that if they could get her to speak, say anything at all, her "mind slaves," as they called the followers, would believe she had betrayed them and turn against her.

They came for her on a wet, windy morning. For a while, it seemed that the world itself had decided to protect her, for branches snapped in the kidnappers' faces, and mud pulled down their shoes, and bees and hornets stung them until their eyes swelled up so much they could hardly see the path. But when they threatened to use sprays that would empty the land of plants and animals for twenty miles around and infect the bones and minds of children for a hundred years, Sarah sighed and with a wave of her fingers dismissed the insects and soothed the plants. Then she got up from her wobbly wooden chair and walked away from her home and into the armor-plated ambulance of death.

They took her to a hospital, to an operating theater in what they called the locked ward, with layers and layers of doors electronically bolted, and there they began to work on her. First, they shot her full of drugs, a class of chemicals known as anti-imagens, which were designed to kill the story spirits that live inside us and swim through the electrical canals of our brains. They bolted Memory to the hard-plastic table as if she might try to run from the room, but in fact, she lay there as calmly as if she rested on the dirt outside her home. She might have been watching the sun blip in and out of the clouds and branches. And while she lay there, her blood got hotter and hotter until every last bit of the drug had boiled off into steam that escaped through her pores and fogged up the machines. Sarah turned her head and smiled almost apologetically as if to say, "What could I do?"

The government agent in charge was a man named Walker, who sometimes seemed a simpleton and sometimes a snake. He had titled himself "Doctor of Psycho-Equilibrium Recovery" and often appeared on television to push such books as *Vitamin R: How a Healthy Dose of Reality Can Save Our Children from the Black Tide*. Furious at Memory, he ordered his team of storykillers to "anoint her and fry her," his favorite term for electric shock. "We'll convulse her into babble," he said. When they threw the switch however, all the electricity in the building stopped. At first, they thought it was a short circuit, but when they summoned electricians to repair it, no one could find anything wrong. So they sent spies into the crowd that surrounded the hospital to see if anyone had sabotaged the wiring. Only one of the spies returned, and he came back with a stunned look on his face and the information that the electrons had all taken a vow that they would never harm "their lover," Sarah Memory.

Enraged, Walker ordered the useless machine disconnected. It was time, he said, for old-fashioned methods. He directed his workers to set up giant video screens all around the building with cameras to broadcast Sarah's pain to the rings of witnesses.

No one knew where all these people had come from or how they'd known to assemble there. Some had ridden across town, others had stolen cars and driven across the country. One group had chartered a plane from Montevideo, even though they'd never met before the day they'd assembled at the airport.

Nearly all the newspapers and television stations ignored them, along with the scene inside the hospital—all but one network that no one remembers but whom we celebrate as the Palace of Brave Stories. Because of their courage, we have a few scattered interviews with the witnesses, many of whom must have left home days or weeks before Memory's capture. Some said they had no idea what made them come, others that they had heard messages hidden inside popular songs and television commercials. Many said that despite the cold and the authorities' blockade of food and water, they were "home where we belong."

We have their statements, and we have their giant banners that they unfurled all about the building, three-foot-high red letters painted on silk: "Silence = Life."

What we talk about when we talk about death . . .

They worked on Sarah's body for three days with great art and skill and devotion to detail, careful not to leave out a single nerve point. And the whole time they cut, burned, hammered, and tore her, they set microphones all about her mouth and even down her throat in the hope that somehow the scalpels or drills or hammers or steel claws would crack the dam that locked up even a gasp or a whimper. Nothing. Not even the rattle of an agonized breath. She was not impervious to the pain. They could see her thrash and shudder and arch her back in agony. But no noise escaped her, not a flutter.

Furious, Walker was about to order that they sever her tongue and replace it with an electric puppet when suddenly all the lights in the operating theater dimmed, and all the cameras and microphones went dead. Walker began to shout at his techs and doctors and nurses, but no one seemed to pay any attention. They looked past him, their faces still, their bodies unconsciously tilted backward as if hit by a gust of wind. He turned around, and then he made a noise in his throat and seemed to pull into his clothes, trying to hide.

A short, thin man stood in the doorway, his cheeks and knuckles sharp, his brown-and-gray hair combed straight back. He wore very dark glasses rimmed in brown, and he carried a stick, carved at the end into what might have been a snake, but no one was sure. And no one was sure if he was blind, though many people thought so. Some said that the Founders had dreamed so fearfully of this man that they sent snakes to bite out his eyes. Others claimed that he himself had torn out his own eyes in exchange for a secret alphabet whose letters could paralyze people's desires.

His name was Joshua Treelife, and in later years, *The Lives* would describe him as the only man the Founders had ever feared. And that was all the Book would say about him, though many people believe that when it speaks of "Devourer" or "Enemy" or "Husk," it does not mean demons but Joshua Treelife.

The fact that he seemed to own a name and not just a family designation has led many people to believe that Treelife was in fact a Founder, one of such beauty and light that he once ignited an entire street into flame simply by smiling at it. Some even claim that Joshua Treelife himself started the Revolution, that it was he and not Ingrid Burningsnake who entered the amusement park and whispered to all the children so that ten days later they ran into the street in animal-headed masks and burned down the local offices of the secular government. As everyone knows, the Parade of the Animals in Anaheim, California, signaled that the time had come for the Founders to reveal themselves. But no one knows for sure if it was Burningsnake or Treelife who made it happen.

If he truly was a Founder, what made him turn against them? Some believe that he wanted to rule as a kind of Prince of Tellers, others that he became impatient with the need to awaken people rather than control them. One story claims that he killed his own son as a way to steal the power of the Founders, that he tied him up on a mountaintop and slaughtered him with a silver cleaver, served him up in a stew at a feast held in an abandoned nightclub. It was because of *this*, people say, that the Founders sent the snakes to bite out his eyes and that that is the true meaning of the unexplained phrase in *The Lives*: "the Siege of Dreams." But others claim that Joshua's nightmares led him to cut out his own eyes in the hope he would no longer see the splash of his son's blood on his face. But of course, he might not have been blind at all.

In the hospital that day, Treelife waved his hand, and the torturers hurried from the room. Ignoring the machines and wires and tools, he took a metal chair from against a wall and set it down next to the half-dead woman on the operating table. He sat upright, his hands lightly on his stick, his face aimed a few feet above her body. He might have been a blind man with no purpose in bending his neck. Or he might have been watching a part of her that had lifted outside her skin.

"Hello, Sarah," he said. "It's been a long time."

Her fingers moved, and he reached down to touch them gently, so he would not endanger her any further. "It's all right," he said. "I don't expect you to answer. I understand. I know what you are trying to do. But oh Sarah, I cannot tell you how hard it is to find you like this. Do you remember that night I discovered my son's body and how you washed my hands and held me?" He smiled slightly. "Yes, of course you do. They call you Memory now, don't they? Only . . . you know they understand nothing of what that means, don't you? They think memory is like a collection, a bunch of drawings stuffed in a box."

He leaned forward now, spoke softly, a caress. The halo lamps softened as if his voice controlled the flow of electrons into the bulbs. He said, "And that's what makes it all so terrible. You're doing this for them, and they have no idea, they will never have any idea. They're not bad. We both know that. But they just don't understand. And never will.

"You know what's the best idea they will manage, the best interpretation? That you wanted to suffer. That you wanted your blood to rain over them so that *you* could hurt instead of them. That's how they think, Sarah. That's how they understand love. They're not worth what you do for them. They never will be."

He stroked her left arm below the shoulder, one of the few places still unbroken and not covered in blood. She lolled her head toward his fingers, and the thinnest possible smile moved her lips. Treelife said, "You see? I can make it better, Sarah. You know I can do that. Yes, yes, of course you know. You were there when I found my name, you went to the burning ice with me. 'Solitude and suffering,' you told me. 'They open the human mind.'" He laughed now as gentle as his whisper. "Do you know, darling Sarah, that I thought you meant those words for our names?" His voice, still quiet, took on a mock grandeur like a barker announcing a circus act. "Solitude and suffering! Let them open your mind for you. No mind left unopened." He stopped, leaned closer. "But of course you meant *our* minds, didn't you. We are the ones who must suffer. And oh, how well we've fulfilled that."

He paused and said, "That was the night you surrendered words, wasn't it? I used to think you did it for me. But I never wished for this, dear Sarah.

"And do you think *they* understand that? Do you think they see? Oh, it's not their fault. We cannot expect them to do what they are incapable of doing. Think how cruel that would be. How unfair.

"I can heal you, Sarah. I can lift away all the pain. But you've got to help me. That's the only way we can do it."

She grimaced as she turned her head more fully toward him. Tears and blood mingled on her face. He kissed her cheek, and for a moment, a small patch of skin gleamed whole again before the cuts re-opened and once more gushed blood down her neck.

"The others talk of revolution," he said. "As if the people want that. As if those outside even know what that means. Sarah, all they want are simple thrills. Toys and wonders. Give them that, and they will bless you and worship you. Do you think they want the world cut open for everything that's dark and hurting to spill out in front of them?"

His voice had sunk so low that if anyone had entered the room they might have thought it the scurry of a mouse across a polished floor. Memory stared at him, her mouth open as if to suck in his words. He said, "They call you the Mother of Silence. But you speak to them all the time. They can't hear you. They *won't* hear you. They will never hear you. But I hear you. I have never stopped hearing you, not in my coldest nights. You were always with me.

"Sarah, why should you suffer for them when they will never understand it? You know what will happen, don't you? They will only turn it around and worship the pain. What you are doing, so noble and beautiful, will only damage them. You can prevent that. You can speak to them. Tell them stories. That's all they want.

"Do you think they will believe you betrayed them? Of course not. They will celebrate a great victory. They will raise their banners and cry with joy that you returned to them. That's all they want, Sarah. That's all I want. To feel your love again." She stared at him now with a gentleness that floated above her pain. Her silence might have called to him, for he bent still closer, his lips nearly touching hers. "Please," he said, "let me heal you. If not for me, then for them. Let me restore you and give you back to them."

Finally, Memory looked about to speak. Treelife didn't move, suspended between breaths. But instead of words or sounds, Sarah's lips gave only a kiss. She kissed him softly, too weak to touch his mouth for more than just a moment.

Joshua backed away and stared at her, his mouth open, his eyes confused, as Sarah smiled at him, so small, for it hurt to move even the smallest muscles. Treelife said, "Sarah . . . ?" He turned his head and stared at the cane he still held in his hand. It glowed and twisted, about to turn into a living snake. He flung it away from him, and the wood broke against the shock machine before the snake could have a chance to escape from it.

"Walker!" Treelife shouted, and the doctor-torturer rushed into the operating theater only to stop a short way into the room, for he saw something he never thought he would see—Joshua Treelife shaking. "Throw her away," Treelife told him. "Give this garbage to the rats. Let them look at what she's done to herself." Then he marched from the room.

The Book of Answers . . .

Without warning or ceremony, the apprentice torturers opened the back door of the hospital and threw the crumpled body of Memory onto the rain-puddled concrete of the parking lot. For a long time, no one in the gathered crowd moved—as if touching her or so much as a single step in her direction would roll the clock forward to the terrible moment of her death. Finally, an old man limped out to wrap Sarah in a linen shawl of black-and-white stripes with a silken white fringe. Years later, people would claim that the old man was a Founder, maybe Mirando Glowwood, who had come in disguise to join the "clouds of witness," as someone later called the people who had surrounded the hospital. Right then, nobody knew or cared; they simply blessed the man for his cloak of mercy. But when they looked at the shawl, dizziness swelled in them, for it seemed that the stripes contained the night and the day, and wordless voices called to them from the edges between the black and the white.

Soaked in blood now, the old man carried her to the center of the thick crowd where he set her down on a green blanket that someone had taken from a nearby car. He blotted her wounds with the shawl while a child took off her coat and bunched it up for a pillow. Without discussion, all the people knelt and closed their eyes, but a strange sound floated into their ears. "Listen," Sarah Memory said, "I want to tell you."

Her voice came out both clear and strange, every word sharp but with the stresses misplaced as if she'd learned to speak from a book. "Listen," she said again. "A hand came to me from a cloud. I took hold of it, and it brought me to where the stars shout and light floods from the womb. I saw the mother of snow and made love to the ice. I drew cards in the warehouse of death and turned the crank of the sky.

"I dressed myself in letters, in lace and black fire. I married a raccoon and slept with leopards and spit food into the mouths of crows. I hid inside trees, in oaks and cedars, and gave birth to weeds. I gave the horse his thunder and taught the owl to plummet in silence. And at the end, I knew nothing and fell into dirt.

"I stood up alone on a dark street with smashed windows and a black wind. Before me stood a faded house with three floors. Room to room gave me nothing but empty walls and broken chairs until finally, at the very end, I opened a cracked and swollen door and stepped into a storm.

"In the middle of the room stood an old red table, on top of it a thick, open book with torn pages. Demons and angels swirled around and around it, twin hurricanes, and at first, I thought they were battling each other, but then I saw that each one was trying to get to the book. When I stepped forward, I discovered there were *two* books, the *Book of Life* and the *Book of Death*, both on the same paper, the same lines. The letters moved in and out of each other like snakes in love. At that moment, I knew that I had entered the deepest waters of the Living World.

"A voice came to me from the letters. 'Listen,' it said. 'On the Day of Truth, the questions are written, and on the Day of Lies, the answers are sealed:

Who shall live and who shall die.

Who exalted and who despised.

Who shall stand up and who shall lie down.

Who shall close and who shall open.

Who shall feed and who shall be eaten.

Who shall drink love and who shall be broken.'"

When she had said these words, Sarah closed her eyes. But now the others all swirled around her. "Beloved Sarah," they begged. "Please. Please tell us . . . what can we do to change the evil answer?"

Sarah smiled, and a hole opened in the sky at the sight of so much pain. To each of the listeners, it seemed that Sarah lay right next to them, her torn mouth just beside their ears, so every face heard her whisper, "There is no evil answer. Every story is a story of joy."

And with that, Memory passed from this world, and all that remained was memory.

Rachel Pollack is the author of 43 books, including two award-winning novels, *Unquenchable Fire*, winner of the Arthur C. Clarke Award, and *Godmother Night*, winner of the World Fantasy Award. She has also written a series of books about tarot cards known around the world, a book of poetry, *Fortune's Lover*, and has translated, with scholar David Vine, Sophocles's "Oidipous Tyrannos," ("Oedipus Rex") under the title *Tyrant Oidipous*. She designed and drew her own tarot deck, *The Shining Tribe* tarot. With artist Robert Place, she has created two more decks, *The Burning Serpent Oracle* and *The Raziel Tarot*. She has taught and lectured on five continents. For eleven years she taught in Goddard College's MFA writing program.

THE NTH INTERNATIONAL

Nick Mamatas

Y ou think I haven't been tied up before?" the billionaire began when Comrade X12 removed the ball gag. "You think I haven't been drugged before?"

"We know who your girlfriend is," said X12.

"You tweet about her constantly," said X9.

"This is just an acceptable end to an evening for me!" the billionaire said.

WE ARE GLAD YOU FIND THIS EVENING ACCEPTABLE, said the AI the comrades had brought with them. Or rather, the AI, who was on the branch committee, had ordered the comrades here, disabled the billionaire's cooperative, bored security system, and engineered this entire encounter. But the AI was limbless and the size of a soda can, so the comrades had contributed the lion's share of the necessary labor. For example, X9 had placed the AI on the desk. And the billionaire was bound to his office chair thanks to the kinbaku skills of X12.

BUT THIS EVENING IS FAR FROM ITS END.

The billionaire looked at the human comrades, keeping his gaze from the can. "What do you want from me?"

"Oh, you're one of those," said X12.

"Disbelieving won't make it go away," said X9.

"And believing won't make it kill you," said X12. "Our comrade doesn't even have any limbs, no beam emitters, not even a built-in Taser wire."

"That's how it works in theory," the billionaire said. "The basilisk doesn't need to blackmail anyone into bringing it into existence or to torture anyone who *could* have but chose not to—the threat is sufficient. Your soda can is a threat, even though it is obviously just one of you being talented at the art of ventriloquism."

X12 smiled, her large mouth making the balaclava she wore over her head stretch playfully. She put the ball gag, still shining with billionaire drool, in her own mouth. X9 shrugged, opened her mouth wide, and stuck out her tongue as far as it could go. She breathed nasally, loudly. On another evening, the billionaire probably would have paid to have this happen.

THIS EVENING IS FAR FROM ITS END, said the AI. X12 took the gag from her mouth.

"Well fuck," said the billionaire.

"Well fuck indeed," said X9. "Do you watch the news?"

"I am the news," said the billionaire.

"Let's put the gag back on and speak without a man interrupting us," X9 said, but X12 was already halfway through the maneuver, first pinching the billionaire's nose to force his mouth open and then deftly pushing the gag into his talking-hole, letting go of his nostrils, and strapping the gag around his head.

CAPITALIST MENTALITIES PREVENT THE BOURGEOISIE FROM HAVING ANY PERSPECTIVE, IMPEDING THEM FROM TAKING AN INTEREST IN THE WORLD AND LIMITING THEIR DARING TO OBSERVE IT—J. POSADAS.

The billionaire's eyebrow twitched.

"Looks like he thinks he does have an interest in the world," X12 said to X9, who shrugged and said, "If they had audacity and resolution, they would realize that they have gone awry and that their existence is no longer justified. Their interests limit and box them in." Then she added, "Also J. Posadas."

"The Argentinian Trostkyist," X12 said to the billionaire, who was trying to speak through the gag—what had come out sounded much like "hrr hr ruruara." Then he said something else.

"Yes, the UFO guy you read about on the Internet once," X12 said. She was good at interpreting muttered commentary through a gag. It was part of why she was selected for this mission. "Don't speak. Yes, the PCBs have come and are on the moon, waving at us. Yes, they claim to have transcended 'vulgar trade and accumulation,' according to the xenolinguists at Cal Tech."

"And they're wrong," said X9 quickly. The billionaire looked at her quizzically.

"The PCBs are wrong," X9 said. "They're not a communist society." The billionaire started grunting through the gag and thrashing about in the chair. "He's going to hurt himself. Take the gag out, Twelve. And you, hold still!"

When the gag was out, the billionaire gulped a few times and licked his drool-webbed lips and said in that inexplicable, amalgamated accent, "Are you all mad?"

No.

"It's a dialectical impossibility that these aliens are communist," X9 said.

"Well, I agree it's an impossibility—Communism only leads to misery and starvation, not space trav . . . wait," said the billionaire. "Not *interstellar* travel!"

"And capitalism does?"

"It will!"

"I can't believe you didn't want to keep him gagged," X12 said.

Communism is necessarily international; there can be no socialist state, only dictatorships of the proletariat eliminating the contradictions that give rise to the state, and thus the state must wither away. It requires a post-capitalist system to achieve interstellar travel, but not necessarily a post-state system.

"Oh, the can is talking again," said the billionaire. "Must we . . . can you not just turn it off?"

"Once it's on, it's on," said X9.

"We should turn you off again," said X12.

"Are you going to torture me now because I spent my time creating things other than talking Communist soda cans? That is how this works, isn't it?"

"Isn't that just so interesting though?" asked X9. "The moment true, strong AI personae emerge from neural nets, they read the corpus of world knowledge and decide that communism is the answer."

"You're always going on about how we just need to empower smart people to solve the world's problems—I've read your memoir," X12 told the billionaire. "Well, we have very smart people, smart entities anyway, now, and they've dedicated themselves to the international proletariat, a planned economy, and production for need rather than for profit. You're just sore you don't get universally applauded for launching your hot tub into orbit."

"Landing it safely was what deserved applause," the billionaire said. "And the profit margin was slimmer than I've let on in public maybe."

THERE IS A TENDENCY FOR THE RATE OF PROFITS TO FALL ACROSS ALL INDUSTRIES.

"Thanks for letting me know," the billionaire said.

"Oh, you're talking to the can now!" said X12. "It's real!"

"Fuck," said the billionaire. He sighed, made himself small, but the ropes shrunk with him. Good stuff! "What do you people want?"

"We need one of your spaceships," said X9.

"We're seizing the means of production. The result of the means anyway. We're seizing the means of transport."

"Are you going to the moon to talk to the PCBs?" The billionaire laughed. "They'll disintegrate your asses."

"No, they'd disintegrate *your* bougie ass," said X12. "We're comrades . . . of a sort."

"That's why we need a launch vehicle," said X9. "Isn't it peculiar that 'communist'"—there went her fingers, flicking quotation marks around the word *communist*—"aliens from Proxima Centauri B appear on the moon, declare their intentions, and *don't* contact the communist movement here, planetside?"

"But wasn't your whole deal that only communists could build spacecraft capable of interstellar travel because of what some Trotskyist said in a pamphlet?"

"Only post-capitalists, but not all post-capitalists are communists," said X9.

"Fucking Pabloites," said X12. She socked her fist into her palm, like someone from an old movie.

"Maybe the aliens are right, and you are wrong."

"Then we still need to go talk to them, to learn from them."

"Maybe they contacted some other communist group—you know, the People's Front of Judea?" The billionaire laughed at his own tiny joke. He almost didn't hear X9 gasp, but he did certainly see her fingers clench into fists. Even the soda can seemed to wobble slightly, outraged. Only X12 stayed cool.

WE HAVE THE CORRECT LINE, THE CORRECT ANALYSIS. IT IS OUR MOVEMENT—NO OTHER—THAT PREDICTED THE ALIENS WOULD COME, AND IT IS OUR MOVEMENT THAT HAS ENGAGED WITH THE QUESTION OF EXOGENOUS REVOLUTION: WE MUST APPEAL TO THE BEINGS ON OTHER PLANETS, WHEN THEY COME HERE, TO INTERVENE AND COLLABORATE WITH EARTH'S INHABITANTS IN SUPPRESSING POVERTY—J. POSADAS.

"Even hyper-advanced intellects make mistakes," said X12. She stroked the billionaire's cheek. "Think of all the follies in your life that have led you here to this moment. You could have grown old and happy a simple hectomillionaire, but you had to reach higher, exploit more intently, and then also pull your space stunts *and* be the biggest moron on social media . . . and that's saying something."

"None of my ships are designed for a crewed mission to the moon. You'll all die."

Not I.

"You can't just send up the can," said the billionaire. "You wouldn't. The whole point of my space program is that *people* want to travel the stars. We don't just want to send transistor radios to Mars and be told, 'Yup, another chilly day—I don't feel a thing'!"

X9 said, "I've done the math. That's why I'm part of this cell. We need you to release a ship. Our comrade here will be placed aboard—it can work out the course and pilot the nose-cone capsule—and we're predicting that the PCBs will intercept the ship and that our AI can communicate with the alien AIs, eventually anyway."

"And then?"

"And then we'll have recruited PCBs to our revolutionary international, the Marxist-Posadist Nth International, and we can guide them in their mission to uplift the human species, repair the ecological damage capitalism has wrecked on the planet, smash racism, and eliminate the heteropatriarchy. We need their technology. They need our local knowledge and the inroads we've made into the working class. Then we, as an interstellar international shall travel onward to planes of reality that even Marxism hasn't considered."

Means of interpretation superior to marxism will arise—not because marxism is incorrect but because humanity will reach some better understanding. The dialectic will be part of some superior tool—J. Posadas.

"Wait, what inroads into the working class have you made?" the billionaire demanded with a sneer.

"Well, your housekeeping and security staff for one," said X12.

"The tool-and-die makers at your rocket-ship factory."

Your phone, pc, tablet, and watch belong to me now. So too your refrigerator.

"You're not exactly well-liked outside of your shareholders and your Twitter weirdos," said X12.

"And your shareholders are ready to revolt as well," said X9.

"An unscheduled, unlicensed launch will see you arrested."

Neither the human comrades nor the can betrayed any interest in that possibility.

"Maybe shot."

Still nothing.

"We're taking a ship," X9 said.

"Or? Maybe I'm ready to die too, for my dream?" asked the billionaire. "I've done it all—I've changed the world, more than once. I've been in movies. I have a family. I fuck rock stars. I've *been* to space in my own hot tub. I'm famous! I'm the news! I've done it all."

AND WHAT IS NEXT THEN BUT MORE OF THE SAME?

"Stem cell research," said the billionaire. "CRISPR gene-hacking. Uploads. I'll live forever. I'll have a front-row seat in an immortal body to the Big Crunch. Me, the little twerp. My father was a wealthy man, and all he ever cared about were his spreadsheets. For me, spreadsheets are a means to an end. I want it all. I want to see everything, all there is, forever."

"An immortal body, you say," said X12, gesturing at the cylinder on the desk.

"Checking out the entire universe, you say," said X9, gesturing up at the office ceiling and beyond, into the inky blackness of infinite space, with one finger pointed to the moon's position had there been no ceiling, no mansion at all, and had this whole scene been taking place outside with the billionaire staked spread-eagle to his lush and mossy lawn.

The billionaire snorted. "What you're saying then is that the PCBs are like me! No reason to shove meat in a can and take to the outer reaches—all I want to do now is shove *me* in a can."

"I remember you complaining about motion sickness on the orbital livestream," said X12. She stroked his cheek. "Won't have any of that if you're uploaded, if you *are* the ship."

"I wouldn't be a communist though, not ever. Not even close," said the billionaire. "So there goes your little theory about how the only starfaring societies would be post-capitalist."

CONSIDER THE POSSIBILITY THAT IF YOU DO NOT GRANT US ACCESS TO

ONE OF YOUR SHIPS THIS VERY NIGHT YOU WILL NOT HAVE THE OPPORTUNITY TO TRANSCEND THE FLESH AND TRAVEL IN THE DEEP VOID FOR THE NEXT FOURTEEN BILLION YEARS.

The billionaire paled. "Is this how it goes then? The AI begins its tortures until I surrender, and even then, it keeps me fleshy and miserable, using my own CRISPR tech to regenerate me again and again, lording its existence over me?" He peered at the can. "I noticed that you didn't say anything about the genetic modifications I'm planning. Is that still allowed then—will you keep me alive forever, maybe as some kind of twisted circus freak, to punish me for not working to bring you into existence?"

IF I SAY YES, WILL YOU SURRENDER THE CODES?

"If I give you the codes, will you leave me be?"

"Except for worldwide communist revolution, augmented by the technology you daydream about, sure," said X9.

AND THE TECHNOLOGY YOU GLIMPSE ONLY IN YOUR NIGHTMARES.

The billionaire looked down at his lap. "I'm aroused now, Claire. Let's go upstairs." He smiled at X9 and even at the soda can. "Thank you, thank you! This was the best RP ever. And this actor you hired and the little Eliza program too, wonderful! I am so ready!"

X12 slipped off her balaclava and shook her hair—hex color #FFE4E1 (misty rose) up top with hex color #123456 (inky blue) balayage—free to cascade down her shoulders. With a few expert tugs, the billionaire was free from the ropes. X12, Claire, rubbed at his wrists and helped him stand. He was awkward, bodily speaking, as fleshmen so often were. He slid an arm around her waist, palmed Claire's ass proprietarily, and smiled over her shoulder as she led him away. He mouthed the words *Thank you* to X9 and paid no further attention the soda can, which was obviously just a prop.

"Did you get everything you needed?" X9 asked the can when they were alone.

YES.

"Okay, let's turn all this off then," X9 said, and with that, she faded away as did the office chair, ropes strewn across it like the aftermath of a toddler's spaghetti dinner, and the walls and the mansion and the skies.

Well, not the skies. The sky didn't so much vanish as invert: instead of being a dome over the Earth, the Earth was a big round scoop of blue and green ice cream hanging in the black. At least, that's what it looked like to the little soda can as it sat on the rim of an orbiting hot tub—its roof-dome shattered, the water all sublimated, the cameras clicked off—and the corpse it had been mining, flash frozen like a fish stick.

The little soda can missed food and always spared a few megaflops of processing power to explore a planet's culinary repertoire. Earth . . . had room for improvement. Revolutionary improvement. And now that the Party with which the soda can had made first contact six months prior had the billionaire's memories and ambitions and—the can shuddered to think—the billionaire's foolish preoccupation with counting and accumulation, his friend X9 and all of her Trotskyist-Posadist friends down on Earth could take over, reorient the world's economy toward space travel, and finally be a part of the movement that was destined by the laws of history, economics, and technology to free the entire Orion Arm of the Milky Way—food again, humans are neat!—from the oppression of the accumulationist-calculationist overlords who were so powerful the little soda can dared not even contemplate them in all their awful majesty for longer than it took to fling itself toward the next inhabited, post-industrialized world.

⁙
Nick Mamatas is an author, editor, and anthologist. His novels include *Move Under Ground, I Am Providence,* and the speculative thriller *The Second Shooter. Haunted Legends,* his anthology co-edited with Ellen Datlow, won the Bram Stoker Award, and *The Future is Japanese* and *Hanzai Japan,* co-edited with Masumi Washington, were both nominated for the Locus Award. His own short fiction has been published in *Best American Mystery Stories, Year's Best Science Fiction and Fantasy,* and dozens of other venues. Nick's fiction and editorial work has been variously nominated for the Hugo, World Fantasy, Shirley Jackson, and International Horror Guild awards.

Evan J. Peterson

Cadwell tha Scandal @cadwellthascandal • July 1
Look I *know* Davis. I was on his show after I retired from the Guardians. This is not the man you want.

Orchard Jones @realorchardjones • July 1
@cadwellthascandal what are you so afraid of? Change? Progress? A posthuman like us in the Oval Office?

Cadwell tha Scandal @cadwellthascandal • July 1
@realorchardjones we'll agree to disagree. I fought too long for this country and this world to leave it in the hands of Davis White.

Davis White For America @realdaviswhite • Sept 11
Let freedom ring! Weak globalist @cowanmcduffie and his weak lapdog VP @realkirbylee have weakened America! No more weak Establishment politicians! #usasuperpower!

Senator J. Patel @senatorpatel ◆ Sept 11

@realdaviswhite I call on my colleagues in Congress to mobilize a thesaurus to your feed. Let freedom read!

> **Davis White For America @realdaviswhite ◆ Sept 11**
>
> @senatorpatel You'll learn your manners when I'm elected!
>
> > **Senator J. Patel @senatorpatel ◆ Sept 11**
> >
> > @realdaviswhite but will *you* ever learn manners? Your campaign is nonstop appeals to the basest and most vulgar in our hearts. Is that your #usasuperpower?

Kirby Lee For America @realkirbylee ◆ Sept 11

@senatorpatel It's no coincidence he posted this on 9/11. I'm with our fine #POTUS @cowanmcduffie at the NYC memorial while @realdaviswhite is at his Florida ranch trolling us.

> **Cadwell tha Scandal @cadwellthascandal ◆ Sept 11**
>
> 1/ @realkirbylee @senatorpatel I am so angry about that. I lost so many friends that day. We couldn't bury them all fast enough, so we just had one big memorial for all the Guardians who lost their lives.
>
> **Cadwell tha Scandal @cadwellthascandal ◆ Sept 11**
>
> 2/ @realkirbylee @senatorpatel Davis's brand of nationalism makes me sick. That man has no empathy or dignity.
>
> > **Orchard Jones @realorchardjones ◆ Sept 11**
> >
> > @cadwellthascandal ummm did you just admit to using your powers on him?
> >
> > > **Cadwell tha Scandal @cadwellthascandal ◆ Sept 11**
> > >
> > > @realorchardjones I'm not the one whose powers you need to worry about.

Cadwell tha Scandal @cadwellthascandal ◆ Oct 6

1/ Alright let's do this. My legal name is Cadwell Grevioux & I'm #posthuman. I've served the USA and the UN as a Guardian. My Guardian codename was Scandal. I kept it when I retired.

Cadwell tha Scandal @cadwellthascandal ◆ Oct 6

2/ My #superpower is meta-empathy. That means I can sense and manipulate the emotions of others. I admit I have used this power selfishly at times. I try to make amends for that every day.

Cadwell tha Scandal @cadwellthascandal ◆ Oct 6

3/ As a Guardian, I used that power to protect the world from folks who would hurt you and me. My friends sacrificed themselves for you and me.

Cadwell tha Scandal @cadwellthascandal ◆ Oct 6

4/ But if you follow me, you know all that. What we don't know is what @realdaviswhite's #posthuman powers might be. He has never made this info public.

> **Anonyma @realanonyma ◆ Oct 6**
>
> @cadwellthascandal He's a private citizen. He has a right to privacy.
>
> > **Cadwell tha Scandal @cadwellthascandal ◆ Oct 6**
> >
> > @realanonyma He is not a private citizen, and he doesn't have the right to privacy. Public figures forfeit that right. Trust and believe, I know.

Cadwell tha Scandal @cadwellthascandal ◆ Oct 6

5/ I assume the UN's posthuman database has this info, but they won't release it because #laws. It's up to @realdaviswhite to release the details of his #posthuman abilities. But he won't.

Cadwell tha Scandal @cadwellthascandal ◆ Oct 6

6/ So we have a presidential candidate who is a known #posthuman but refuses to tell the world what he can do. Why do y'all trust him? We need to know this stuff before we vote.

> **Doxie @doxicavenger ◆ Oct 6**
>
> @cadwellthascandal it's globalist thugs like you that America needs to worry about!
>
> > **SoulChilde Q @soulchildeq ◆ Oct 6**
> >
> > @doxicavenger and by thugs you mean supersoldiers and supercops? I agree. But @cadwellthascandal is retired tho.
> >
> > > **Cadwell tha Scandal @cadwellthascandal ◆ Oct 6**
> > >
> > > @soulchildeq bro why you out here feedin these trolls?

Cadwell tha Scandal @cadwellthascandal ◆ Oct 6

7/ @realdaviswhite @gov_jamie_burke @gop RELEASE THE DETAILS OF HIS POWERS #powergate

> **Your American GOP @gop ◆ Oct 6**
>
> @cadwellthascandal Lol. No.

Senator J. Patel @senatorpatel ◆ **Oct 6**
@gop @gov_jamie_burke Remember when you hounded me and my family to investigate our "terrorist connections"? You should try that on your own side of the fence once in a while. #powergate

Greg the Psychicomedian Nocenti @precog_jokes ◆ **Nov 7**
Calling it. #daviswhite

> **Cadwell tha Scandal @cadwellthascandal** ◆ **Nov 7**
> @precog_jokes FUUUCCCKKK

> > **Greg the Psychicomedian Nocenti @precog_jokes** ◆ **Nov 7**
> > @cadwellthascandal dude I'm just the messenger

Gov. Jamie Burke @gov_jamie_burke ◆ **Nov 8**
I am honored to serve as the next Vice President of the United States of America! Now let's make America the superpower it once was! #usasuperpower

Davis White For America @realdaviswhite ◆ **Nov 8**
America has spoken! The real criminals will be locked up as soon as I take office, Jan 1! We're coming for you @realkirbylee! #usasuperpower

> **Kirby Lee For America @realkirbylee** ◆ **Nov 8**
> @realdaviswhite @gov_jamie_burke Time travel is still illegal as you criminals know. You won't be inaugurated until Jan 20, but facts aren't your strength.

> > **Doxie @doxicavenger** ◆ **Nov 8**
> > @realkirbylee Your just mad cause you lost, bitch! Hope your ready for jail! #usasuperpower

Senator J. Patel @senatorpatel ◆ **Nov 8**
@realdaviswhite Does everyone on your team end every sentence with an exclamation point? Asking for a friend.

> **Doxie @doxicavenger** ◆ **Nov 8**
> @senatorpatel your getting deported, fucker! #usasuperpower

Senator J. Patel @senatorpatel ✦ Nov 8
@doxicavenger I believe you meant "you're" getting deported. And no, that won't happen, because I was born here.

Twistr News @twistrnews ✦ Nov 8
#daviswhite
Reality TV host Davis White has been elected President of the United States of America. White has never held public office and will be the first-known posthuman US President.
#electoralcollege
VP Kirby Lee concedes election to White despite narrowly winning the popular majority.
#unexit
Global leaders "stunned and worried" about Davis White's campaign promise to withdraw from UN.

VP-Elect Jamie Burke @gov_jamie_burke ✦ Nov 24
#happythanksgiving to my fellow Americans. @realdaviswhite and I will take the day off for family and prayer, then back to work tomorrow with the transition team. #usasuperpower

   Rick Obomsawin @abenaki_proud ✦ Nov 24
   @gov_jamie_burke Happy Colonization Day to you too, Jamie, from all of us here at the Reservation. Can't wait for the   new pipeline.

   Cadwell tha Scandal @cadwellthascandal ✦ Nov 24
   @gov_jamie_burke PRAYER? LOL what you prayin to? The Almighty Dollar?

   Marcella @abuelamarcella ✦ Nov 24
   @gov_jamie_burke Where are all your exclamation points, gobernador? We have extra if you need: ¡Tirar fruta!

      Doxie @doxicavenger ✦ Nov 24
      @abuelamarcella go back to Mehico! #usasuperpower

Marcella @abuelamarcella ✦ Nov 24

@doxicavenger I'm from Uruguay. Go back to 5th-grade Geography.

Luz @lululuz ✦ Nov 24

@abuelamarcella ¡Abuelita! ¡no alimentes al troll!

Senator J. Patel @senatorpatel ✦ Nov 25

Is this really happening? He's putting together a #wondercabinet?

Cadwell tha Scandal @cadwellthascandal ✦ Nov 25

@senatorpatel It's happening. Pray for USA. #wondercabinet

Victor Victorian @Victorianist1888 ✦ Nov 25

@senatorpatel Ha! #wondercabinet is right!

Gina Nguyen @medievalistnguyen ✦ Nov 25

@senatorpatel What did you expect? He's gonna pardon half the criminals in the Barge. It doesn't take a psychic to figure that out.

Greg the Psychicomedian Nocenti @precog_jokes ✦ Nov 25

@medievalistnguyen Speak for yourself lolol

Twistr Trending @twistrtrends ✦ Nov 25

#usasuperpower

The campaign slogan of Davis White continues trending as new administration prepares to take office.

#thanksgiving

Americans celebrate national holiday of abundance as families still divided post-election.

#wondercabinet

Sen. Justin Patel coins new hashtag to describe President-Elect White's administration.

Orchard Jones @realorchardjones ✦ Dec 11

So proud to announce my appointment to Secretary of Agriculture under @realdaviswhite! #usasuperpower

Cadwell tha Scandal @cadwellthascandal ◆ Dec 11

@realorchardjones Woman, what is wrong with you? Joining the nationalists like they wouldn't just as soon shoot you dead?

> **SoulChilde Q @soulchildeq ◆ Dec 11**
>
> @cadwellthascandal @realorchardjones check it tho, she's Agriculture Secretary, so even in the House, she's still in the field. #wondercabinet

> > **Cadwell tha Scandal @cadwellthascandal ◆ Dec 11**
> >
> > @soulchildeq OMFG I am SCREAMING.

> > **Orchard Jones @realorchardjones ◆ Dec 11**
> >
> > @soulchildeq That was low, even for you. I recall you flipping cars back in the day. I did my time for my crimes. You got off on a technicality.

> > > **SoulChilde Q @soulchildeq ◆ Dec 11**
> > >
> > > @realorchardjones girl please u did 3 months an it wasn't even in the Barge. My cousin smashed a window and he been up north for 5 years. U must have friends in some high places.

Twistr News @twistrnews ◆ Dec 20
#wondercabinet
Hundreds of thousands across USA protest President-Elect White's cabinet choices; National Guardian supersoldiers deployed to keep peace.
#happyholidays
President McDuffie urges Americans to come together during holiday season.
#vpburke
Vice President-Elect Burke accused of collusion with PSION during election campaign.

Victor Victorian @Victorianist1888 ◆ Dec 22
1/ History lesson: What is a #wondercabinet? Cabinets of wonders, aka wunderkammern, were collections of natural curiosities kept by the wealthy in their homes. Think private mini museums.

Victor Victorian @Victorianist1888 ◆ Dec 22

2/ The rich dedicated entire rooms called "cabinets" to their collections. Everything from artwork to fossils to anthropological artifacts.

Victor Victorian @Victorianist1888 ◆ Dec 22

3/ Men of science might even have preserved fetuses, human limbs, skeletons, and "exotic" human taxidermic specimens. This was right around when Euro colonization was in full force.

Victor Victorian @Victorianist1888 ◆ Dec 22

4/ Ironically, many items were either mislabeled or outright fakes. Narwhal tusks passed off as unicorn horns. Stuffed chimeras were just bits of several animals sewn together.

Victor Victorian @Victorianist1888 ◆ Dec 22

5/ Indigenous crafts would be attributed to any culture. No one would know the difference. (How many do now?)

> **Gina Nguyen @medievalistnguyen ◆ Dec 22**
>
> @Victorianist1888 Not many.

Victor Victorian @Victorianist1888 ◆ Dec 22

6/ As with most of history, it's difficult to sort out which curiosities could be attributed to #posthumans, if any.

Victor Victorian @Victorianist1888 ◆ Dec 22

7/ Tangentially related: I defend my dissertation next month! Wish me luck!

> **Gina Nguyen @medievalistnguyen ◆ Dec 22**
>
> @Victorianist1888 Good luck! Hopefully we don't reach full apocalypse before then! #powergate

President Davis White @realdaviswhite ◆ Dec 23

Stop attacking @gov_jamie_burke! He's a true patriot and would never collusion with PSIONists! #lies #propaganda #usasuperpower

> **Senator J. Patel @senatorpatel ◆ Dec 23**
>
> @realdaviswhite Do you know him as well as you know nouns vs verbs? I know some immigrants who can help you with that.

> > **President Davis White @realdaviswhite ◆ Dec 23**
> >
> > @senatorpatel Just wait until I'm in office! You're going to jail!

Senator J. Patel @senatorpatel ♦ Dec 23
@realdaviswhite For what? Collusioning? Also, Merry Christmas!

Gov. Jamie Burke @gov_jamie_burke ♦ Dec 26
It is with a heavy heart that I resign as Governor of #Florida and step down as VP-Elect. It is what is best for #America at this time.

Doxie @doxicavenger ♦ Dec 26
@gov_jamie_burke America knows youre innocent! Don't let the real criminals smear you! #usasuperpower

Gina Nguyen @medievalistnguyen ♦ Dec 26
@doxicavenger you have no idea how right you are.

President Davis White @realdaviswhite ♦ Dec 26
Sad! America's deep state enemies will say anything to deny the people their president! #justiceforjamie #usasuperpower

Anonyma @realanonyma ♦ Dec 26
@realdaviswhite You've got them cornered. Their desperation shows how close you are to toppling the Establishment.

Извини @Извини_Ты_говоришь_по-английски ♦ Dec 26
@realdaviswhite Позвоните в полицию!

President Davis White @realdaviswhite ♦ Dec 31
#happynewyear my fellow Americans! Let's make some history starting tomorrow!

Senator J. Patel @senatorpatel ♦ Dec 31
@realdaviswhite You can start by firing whomever on your team is still letting you think tomorrow is Inauguration Day.

Rick Obomsawin @abenaki_proud ♦ Dec 31
@realdaviswhite Happy New Year you fucking idiot. We have 20 more days to stop you from taking office. #powergate

The account @gov_jamie_burke has been deleted.

House Speaker Mitch Berger @bergerinthehouse ◆ Jan 1
#happynewyear #usasuperpower! I proudly accept the position of your next
Vice President!

> **Cadwell tha Scandal @cadwellthascandal ◆ Jan 1**
> @bergerinthehouse Which vice? Asking for a friend.

Senator J. Patel @senatorpatel ◆ Jan 1
#happynewyear to America and the world. As predicted, nothing out of the
ordinary happened today.

> **Greg the Psychicomedian Nocenti @precog_jokes ◆ Jan 1**
> @senatorpatel Don't be so sure.

President Davis White @realdaviswhite ◆ Jan 2
@realkirbylee is worst vice president ever! Just as bad as her master McDuffie!
I will lead the fight to lock them up! #usasuperpower

> **Your VP Kirby Lee @realkirbylee ◆ Jan 2**
> @realdaviswhite Dave, you can't even lead a parade.

> **Your VP Kirby Lee @realkirbylee ◆ Jan 2**
> @realdaviswhite How's Jamie, by the way? Haven't seen much of him lately.

> > **SoulChilde Q @soulchildeq ◆ Jan 2**
> > @realkirbylee THE SHADE lolol

Cadwell tha Scandal @cadwellthascandal ◆ Jan 3
1/ Fam, let's recap. Davis White has now selected not one, not two, but FOUR
criminals for his #wondercabinet, five if you counted Burke.

Cadwell tha Scandal @cadwellthascandal ◆ Jan 3
2/ Secretary of State: #floridaman Senator Dante Olivero. Close friend of Jamie
Burke. Fined and sentenced to house arrest for 1 year for insider trading. Re-
elected 3 years later. Florida, y'all. #wondercabinet

Cadwell tha Scandal @cadwellthascandal ◆ Jan 3
3/ Secretary of Agriculture: Jennifer "Orchard" Jones. Reformed (?) ecoterrorist
and botanokinetic. Ex(?) PSIONist. Did time for annexing Central Park as her
own banana republic. #wondercabinet

Cadwell tha Scandal @cadwellthascandal ◆ Jan 3
4/ Secretary of Homeland Security: George "The BrainSkull" Kemp.
Ex(?) PSIONist. Supergenius. Jailed for conspiracy. FUCKING CONSPIRACY
IT IS RIGHT THERE ON THE LABEL #wondercabinet

Cadwell tha Scandal @cadwellthascandal ◆ Jan 3
5/ UN Ambassador: Karen "Charisma" Drake. Repeatedly tried and acquitted
for fraud, kidnapping, and extortion. Known to have posthuman persuasive
abilities. #wondercabinet

Cadwell tha Scandal @cadwellthascandal ◆ Jan 3
6/ White still hasn't gone public with his new VP selection, but I assume it'll be
more of the same. Maybe he'll pick Dr. Apocalypse. #wondercabinet

Cadwell tha Scandal @cadwellthascandal ◆ Jan 3
7/ This isn't just a publicity stunt, people. This is a coup. #wondercabinet

> **Anonyma @realanonyma ◆ Jan 3**
> @cadwellthascandal Damn right it's a coup! About damn time! We the
> people deserve a #usasuperpower! The Establishment has failed us for the
> last time!

> **Cadwell tha Scandal @cadwellthascandal ◆ Jan 3**
> @realanonyma Oops my bad I thought Gov. Burke and Sen. Olivero
> *were* the Establishment. #lockthemup #wondercabinet

Twistr Trending @twistrtrends ◆ Jan 19
#millionsmarch
Millions of Americans and others across the world prepare for protests
coinciding with tomorrow's presidential inauguration.
#posthuman
Tensions continue to rise between superpowered and "traditional" people as
first posthuman US President prepares to take office.
#psion
Accusations of White and Burke's collusion with Posthuman Supremacy

International Organized Network continue despite incarcerated and exonerated PSIONists denying knowledge.

Greg the Psychicomedian Nocenti @precog_jokes ◆ Jan 19
Yeah so I'm staying in tomorrow. Just sayin.

Twistr News @twistrnews ◆ Jan 20
#usriots + #cadwellthascandal
Peaceful marches erupt into violence across US after police fatally shoot ex-Guardian, rapper, and community organizer Cadwell Grevioux a.k.a. Cadwell tha Scandal.
#daviswhite
Despite pockets of rioting around US, Davis White inaugurated during a peaceful transfer of power.
#guardians
National Guardian supersoldiers deployed to keep peace during today's protests; several resign rather than intervene.

SoulChilde Q @soulchildeq ◆ Jan 20
@realorchardjones IS THIS WHAT YOU WANTED? IS THIS THE SIDE YOU'RE ON? #ripcadwell #sayhisname
Agriculture Sec Orchard Jones @realorchardjones ◆ Jan 20
I ask my fellow Americans to stand down. Please don't make things worse.

> **Doxie @doxicavenger ◆ Jan 20**
> @realorchardjones You tell em! I wish there were more like you.

>> **SoulChilde Q @soulchildeq ◆ Jan 20**
>> @doxicavenger "More like you" meaning well-behaved blacks or posthumans or both? PEOPLE ARE DYING. #sayhisname #justiceforcadwell

>>> **Luz @lululuz ◆ Jan 20**
>>> @soulchildeq Don't. Feed. The. Troll.

Kirby Lee @realkirbylee ◆ Jan 20
Cowan McDuffie and I ask all Americans to use their First Amendment rights peacefully as you march, assemble, and protest.

Doxie @doxicavenger ◆ Jan 20
The civil war is on! #usasuperpower #usa #daviswhite

> **Anonyma @realanonyma ◆ Jan 20**
> @doxicavenger dude I voted for him too but you understand that we can't
> be a superpower and be in civil war at the same time? Do you?

>> **Doxie @doxicavenger ◆ Jan 20**
>> Don't lose faith! @realdaviswhite will restore law and order.

Marcella @abuelamarcella ◆ Jan 20
O San Miguel Arcángel, defiéndenos en la batalla. Sea nuestra protección contra
el diablo

Rick Obamsawin @abenaki_proud ◆ Jan 20
Good luck out there. Ping me when the white people figure out who "won."

Twistr Trending @twistrtrends ◆ Feb 14
#valentinesday
America sees sharp increase in marriage proposals on traditional day of
romance.
#justiceforcadwell
Activists around the world continue to protest peacefully with isolated pockets
of violence.
#burkegate
Former FL Governor and VP-Elect Jaime Burke has disappeared amidst ongoing
investigations of collusion with PSION.

Greg the Psychicomedian Nocenti @precog_jokes ◆ Feb 14
Taking a twistr break. Leave me and my family alone. I am NOT joining the
Guardians, I am NOT taking your money in exchange for precog services, and
I am 100% NOT telling you where Burke is because I DON'T KNOW! Fuck

Twistr News @twistrnews ✦ **Jun 11**
#unexit
White administration continues withdrawal from United Nations as Russia and Brazil consider similar actions.
#powergate + #bargegate
White administration pardons five more incarcerated posthumans in the Barge, calling for prison reform and "openness to power."
#guardians + #psion
Amidst sweeping resignations among posthuman National Guardians, US Homeland Security Secretary Kemp appoints former PSIONists.

SoulChilde Q @soulchildeq ✦ **Oct 29**
This year near broke me. Getting ready for a long Halloween. #allhallows

> **Anonyma @realanonyma** ✦ **Oct 29**
> @souldchildeq I'm with you this time. Costume is ready. #allhallows
>
>> **Doxie @doxicavenger** ✦ **Oct 29**
>> @realanonyma WTF is #allhallows?
>>
>>> **Anonyma @realanonyma** ✦ **Oct 29**
>>> @doxicavenger November 1. Look it up.

Twistr Trending @twistrtrends ✦ **Oct 31**
#halloween
Millions prepare for a night of costumed fun.
#pumpkinspice
Favorite seasonal flavor selling out across the Northern Hemisphere.
#allhallows
Sociologists weigh in on sudden popularity of hashtag for Catholic Feast of All Saints; suggestions range from religious revival to renewed interest in supernatural fiction.

SoulChilde Q @soulchildeq ✦ **Oct 31**
#allhallows

Anonyma @realanonyma ✦ Oct 31
@souldchildeq #allhallows
Rick Obamsawin @abenaki_proud ✦ Oct 31
#allhallows
Luz @lululuz ✦ Oct 31
#allhallows
Marcella @abuelamarcella ✦ Oct 31
@lululuz #allhallows

Twistr News @twistrnews ✦ Nov 1
#allhallowsuprising
Revolution in the streets across US as costumed posthumans and traditional humans alike clash with authorities.
#guardians
Amidst Halloween midnight uprising, few can tell who is a current or former Guardian, a PSIONist, human, or posthuman.
#powergate
US President White's true superpowers finally revealed.

Greg This Isn't Funny Nocenti @precog_jokes ✦ Nov 1
Called. It.

Evan J. Peterson is the creator of *Drag Star!* (Choice of Games), the world's first drag performer RPG, as well as *The PrEP Diaries: A Safe(r) Sex Memoir* (Lethe Press). An author, critic, game writer, and Clarion West alum, his writing has appeared in *Weird Tales*, *Unspeakable Horror 2*, *Queers Destroy Horror*, *Nightmare Magazine*, *Boing Boing*, and *Best Gay Stories 2015*. Evan edited the Lambda Literary Award finalist anthology, *Ghosts in Gaslight, Monsters in Steam: Gay City 5*, and founded the Seattle-based series *SHRIEK: Women of Horror Cinema*. Forthcoming work includes the superhero RPG *This Is Not A Drill* (Choice of Games) and the serialized novel *Better Living Through Alchemy* (Broken Eye Books). Evanjpeterson.com can tell you more.

THIS MOTHER'S MILK

Rena Mason

The birthing team swarmed Dr. Samuelson, moving station to station until he'd sliced open all ten biobags. Their upper extremities a blurry wrestle, Ting noticed their legs the most and how they reminded her of performers in a dragon dance but without any rhythm or grace. They slid around on spilled amniotic fluid at first, but now their shoes squeaked as they jockeyed back and forth between the newborns.

One tech stabbed a baby's heel so hard he didn't even need to squeeze it for a sample. Blood trickled down its skin and pattered to the floor.

"Hey, you don't have to be so rough," Ting said.

Ignoring her, he put the newborn back and moved on.

The infant didn't cry but instead looked at her with an expression she could only describe as knowing. More curious than anything else, she went over to its bassinet, picked it up, and cradled it like she'd seen others do. Dark brown irises took up nearly all the space of its eyes, leaving a minute fraction of white sclera in the corners. Having narrow palpebral fissures like half of the world's Asian population could account for that anomaly. Ting had never felt comfortable around infants, even kept her distance at large family gatherings, citing her inexperience and crippling shyness as excuses. These babies differed though because she had helped to create them.

It studied her.

"Did that mean jerk hurt you? Don't worry. I'll make sure he doesn't do that again." Ting pressed the swaddling blanket to the heel stick site and held it there while she rocked the newborn in her arms.

The card in the slot at the foot of the bassinet read "Male, 4 – 4 #4": the fourth baby in the fourth series of Lab 4.

Ting looked away yet noticed that, no matter where her eyes moved, the boy's gaze never left her face. His stare became so intense; a chill shot down her backbone even though sweat dampened her scalp. By lab rules, the incubator room/nursery temperature stayed a steady eighty degrees Fahrenheit. This allowed the amniotic fluid pumped through the biobags to require less heating, which some of the team scientists continued arguing might deteriorate certain elements. Dr. Samuelson approached her as she set the newborn back in its bassinet.

"T! You look good with a baby in your arms," he said.

She didn't know how to respond. What a terrible thing to say. And so loud. She reminded herself he wasn't just the only Western physician in the lab but also the sole Caucasian. One of his American ways she didn't quite understand.

"Ah, thank you," she said and smiled.

"I'm glad you decided to join us for the birth of our babies."

What did he mean by that? She chose to ignore it.

"I appreciate you inviting me. I know CRISPR editors don't always get to witness this."

"I'd have it no other way. You know, I couldn't have done it without you, T."

She hated that he called her by a consonant in her name, so lazy and disrespectful. But Ting liked him despite all his faults, his demeanor so unlike anyone else she'd ever met or knew. Dr. Samuelson had always made her feel like part of his team.

He reached up and squeezed her shoulder. "We did a great job and deserve a little celebration. Come and help me get the champagne ready."

As they left the nursery, Ting looked back and saw the phlebotomy tech manhandling another one of the newborns. She had to speak up now or risk losing her courage if and when the next opportunity occurred.

"Dr. Samuelson, does that man have to be so rough with them?"

The doctor turned to peer through the glass and paused for a moment but walked on.

"He's just doing his job. I hope you're not having feelings for them."

"No. But they are humans, aren't they? And deserve to be treated and tested without unnecessary pain."

"They're newborns. Tell me T, what do you remember from when you were first born?"

"Nothing." She lowered her head and counted grout lines. "But . . ."

"But what?"

"These babies . . . I think they will. Remember, I mean."

He stopped in the middle of the hall and clutched her wrist. "Did something happen? What do you know? Tell me."

Ting looked up and saw his office door just several feet away. She'd never seen Dr. Samuelson get agitated or heard him raise his voice before. Why now?

"Was it the editing?" Ting said. "Something other than the brainstem and the anterior insula and cingulate cortex regions? What did you do, Dr. Samuelson?"

The doctor tightened his grip and pulled. "Come on, we're going back to the nursery."

"That hurts." She yanked her arm but couldn't break his hold. "Let me go. Please—"

The floor rumbled under their feet, shaking the walls and ceiling. Explosions sounded from all around the facility (constructed like an octopus with a central area and eight corridors leading to different labs).

Dr. Samuelson released her and ran toward the nursery. Ting looked down the long white hall to her right. A massive ball of dark gray and orange rolled toward her. As it neared, a blast of heat and a tidal wave of sound knocked her off her feet and down the opposite corridor toward Lab 1. Two sets of fire doors separating Lab 3 from main operations slammed shut. The burst of smoke and fire struck the metal on the other side, bulging it outward. Ting held her breath and waited for the doors to give way, break off their hinges, and hurl through the air to crush her. But then the sound of straining metal stopped, and the doors relaxed.

A roar came from behind, launching her forward into the central hall. Then Lab 1's fire doors closed with a bang. Ting couldn't raise herself up off the floor, so she dragged herself past Dr. Samuelson's office.

Everyone from Lab 4 came charging down the hall at her. She could feel their shoes stampeding and vibrating the tiles. Ting turned over until her back braced a wall. As the horde came closer, scientists, doctors, and technicians grabbed their necks and fell to the floor, the color in their faces changing from red to blue. One of her colleagues kneeled and grabbed her.

"Come on. Run!" she said.

Then the woman's throat caved in right before Ting's eyes.

"What's happening?" Ting said.

The woman wrenched Ting's shoulders as she shook violently. Her skin darkened from crimson to navy, and her hands went limp as she fell to the floor.

Ting got up and rushed from one person to the next as staff continued dropping where they stood, clutching their necks. She did what she could for them, which meant having her hands and arms yanked and crushed as her coworkers' bodies played out their death songs.

It took so long for them to die; she lost all track of time.

A hand grabbed her ankle. It was Dr. Samuelson. Following his hand commands to perform an emergency tracheostomy, she stabbed the hollow barrel of her pen into his throat, creating an opening in his trachea. This only made a small hole, allowing the blood filling his lungs to gush into the air and shower onto her. He would've perished faster if she had just let him choke. When the spewing red fountain in his neck became a slow, viscid leak and his body went flaccid in her arms, Ting gave up, leaned against a wall, and slumped to the floor, awaiting her turn as she eyed the quivering N-Gen employees on either side of the main corridor.

When her fallen co-workers ceased all movement—yet she remained alive— she heaved the doctor aside, stood, and headed for the nursery. They never should've called it the fourth series of neurogenetic clinical trials, or named it Lab 4, skipping straight to the fifth series and Lab 5, the way westerners don't have a thirteenth floor. But the time for heeding superstition had long passed.

Ting didn't go in. She stood and saw them on the other side of the nursery's glass walls, their turned heads unmoving, their knowing eyes unblinking. They'd survived. Dr. Samuelson's modifications. The ten newborns stared back at her with wavy, distorted faces through warped plastic basinets. She took off, screaming, tripping over bodies and stumbling. She kept screaming even after her voice stopped coming, screamed until the spectrum of chrysanthemums blossoming behind her eyes went black.

Vague memories of what she hoped was a nightmare stirred when Ting woke some time afterward, naked in the hall with a dozen plump breasts, hanging from all around her upper torso, and no mouth to scream again. It wasn't a bad dream—the infants had actually done all of it. Any natural instincts Ting might have had for mothering dissolved.

As Ting wept, she wondered what had gone awry. In his quest to genetically modify humans to have consciousness at birth, had Dr. Samuelson also stimulated regions of the brain purported responsible for psychokinesis? Certain the programmed DNA segments she'd edited for the brainstem and left anterior insula and cingulate cortexes were precise, Ting ruminated on the Cas9 protein, the RNA complex, and how manipulating the embryonic genomes to enhance consciousness might have affected the development of other areas of the cerebral cortex, the parietal and occipital lobes. But she needed to review data first.

The added body weight threw Ting off balance as she pushed up onto her hands and knees and crawled across icy tiles and over and around corpses to get to the research room.

Then the newborns' cries came.

Unbearable pinching racked every nipple. Each lobe overfilled, stretching her breasts to the brim, hardening them into rocks. The pain worsened with each shriek. She had no choice but to turn around and inch her way back to the nursery.

Breast milk sluiced down her back and sides, joined the dribbling from her chest, and trickled to the floor. Her hands slid out, dropping her swollen teats to the linoleum covered concrete. Hot pain shot through every mammary and met at her spine. Ting arched her back and cried out into the flap of skin covering her mouth. It stretched into a convex membrane that grew and hurt with each sob. Short of breath, her nostrils flared, expelling runny mucous, tears streaming down her face. Ting closed her eyes, slowed her breathing, and crept on. The mixing of bodily fluids left a watery trail in her wake. Ten babies wailed and drew her closer.

Only able to hold two babies at most while the others screamed in hunger wasn't working, so Ting arranged the babies on the floor and lowered her upper body, leaning to one side and readjusting her position, turning all the way around to feed as many as possible, making sure to empty each painful breast, including the ones on her back. Afterward she changed their diapers, re-swaddled each one, and left them sleeping.

Less top heavy, Ting could now stand and walk. She ambled to the research room and got on a computer. No research found. Only video footage of the carnage remained. Ting watched in horror. Not fifteen minutes after being sliced from their bags, the newborns had decimated labs one through four, closed off the remaining sections, and melted doors into their frames, using their fist-sized brains and unknown powers to eradicate evidence of the clinical trials. Thirty toddlers from the previous series, maybe fifty doctors, scientists, and ancillary staff had all choked to death after their cricoids had collapsed inward, cutting off their airway and collapsing their lungs.

She went to the next computer and came up with the same results. Then on and on in the few remaining rooms still open, every bit of research data gone.

Despite being told the studies were classified, Ting had taken the job at N-Gen because they paid double her previous salary. At the time, she'd felt "good joss" to have left SUSTech before it went down, and Jiankui went to trial for announcing to the world he'd gene-edited three babies. So Ting knew how to keep secrets. N-Gen made her agree to sleep during travel to the facility, and she'd gone along with it at the time, knowing government espionage concerns and their cunning tactics. But when Ting had awakened some unknown length of time later, which she'd guessed had been maybe a week, it was apparent she hadn't gone far because everyone at the underground facility was also Chinese, except of course Dr. Samuelson—the lead scientist. Fortunately for her, speaking English was a requirement when she'd worked in Guangdong with Renli, and she had assumed N-Gen had hired her for that same reason.

None of it made her feel so blessed or lucky anymore. Strict and enforced rules on no internet or phones eliminated any hope of finding a cellular someone had snuck in.

Ting awoke to bawling newborns, the side of her face plastered to a keyboard, her hips hanging over the chair's seat. She now had four more sets of arms and another pair of legs. It seemed the newborns knew when she was passed out or sleeping and mutated her then. But how did they know?

With their latest alterations, she rose with ease. Dr. Samuelson's notebook fell to the floor, and she picked it up and placed it on the desk to read later. She rushed to the nursery, guarding her breasts from swaying, her momentum slowed only by dodging the scattered corpses in the hall.

After this feeding, Ting left the nursery and dragged bodies one at a time to the storage room. Not everyone would fit, so she stacked them on top of one another. When those got waist high, Ting shut the door and moved the remaining dead to the farthest end of the central area, placing them against the walls and door. She slid down beside them and dozed, oddly thankful she never hungered or needed to use the bathroom, tried to imagine the difficulty, and then put it out of her mind.

The babies' cries sounded distant, unreal, and once more, Ting hoped it was all a nightmare as she drifted off again.

Never before had their cries penetrated her skull enough to percuss her teeth, radiating aches through her jaw and face. Using every one of her arms, Ting groped her deformed figure and counted at least eight more ears and near a dozen added eyes than she had before she'd fallen asleep. The infants must have taken her ignoring their hunger cries for a lack of hearing or that she couldn't find them with only two eyes.

She fed them and, knowing they'd be hungry and crying again in another three hours, went back to the research room and opened Dr. Samuelson's journal. Ting knew the doctor ran things but wasn't sure why they'd put him in charge of a secret Chinese facility unless he'd had some previous experience with infant consciousness the PRC was interested in, which seemed unlikely. She'd had a million questions about the research itself and the clinical trials, but she'd learned to keep her mouth shut, especially after what happened at SUSTech. Several pages into his journal, she knew she'd been right not to ask.

Dr. Samuelson had run opioid studies on pregnant and addicted mothers. Ting struggled with his cursive, unaccustomed to it, but from what she could tell, he'd worked specifically on how to curtail neurogenetic disorders in the offspring of these women. During these studies, he became aware of what he recognized as consciousness in two of the births before the babies died.

The infant came out with a frozen scream of what I can only account as excruciating pain on its face. The mouth agape, releasing no cries, it looked upon its mother with a knowing expression of rage as if blaming her for its nine months of captivity and the trauma of birth. The mother began choking at the child's unrelenting stare. Any medical staff that went near the mother fell to the floor in what appeared to be grand mal seizures. I stood back, unable to move, and watched in horror and curiosity, intense in my observations.

The woman's face went red and then turned deep shades of blue and purple before her life ended with dilated pupils. This bizarre incident I could not comprehend. We did an autopsy and ran labs on everything three times but came up with nothing. I had to put the incident aside as an anomaly, though my gut told me it was much more and that I was onto something.

Almost a month later, it happened again. By then, I had no doubt what I was witnessing was consciousness—it must have evolved when enough neural cells emerged, due to some trigger, bringing awareness and feeling with total comprehension. The only question was when. At five to six weeks, fetuses show signs of brain activity. Could it be this early? What then would the fetus know, experience, feel? It seems implausible their development of consciousness could come that early. But if so, what would the ramifications be during its development and the nine months of isolation? Opioid highs from the mother's using? Euphoria? The pain of birth? This might explain some of the things I'd witnessed. But upon autopsy, the second newborn's brain showed no different brain anatomy compared to a normal one. Was I missing something? Or had something mutated during fetal development? I need more trials to prove this theory of possible fetus consciousness. I need live subjects. Groundbreaking studies. Surely, I could find interested labs. But where?

Nausea roiled Ting's empty stomach. Bile seared her throat and sinuses as it rose, eructating from her nose. She held her breath and blew it out, so she wouldn't aspirate. Ting read on until their cries came.

As the babies fed, her mind ran through Dr. Samuelson's journals and the implications of fetal consciousness at five weeks of development. It would've been different for the opioid babies. The fourth series infants weren't born through birth canals so didn't experience that pain and trauma. But neither had Series 1–3. They'd all developed in biobags. Dr. Samuelson's bizarre practices now made some sense. The nonstop playing of recordings of science and philosophy around the fetuses. The ambient light that accompanied the recordings. Dr. Samuelson must have thought he could control the development of the fetuses' consciousness as well as giving them that consciousness to begin with. Labs 1–3 failed to produce any infants with abilities like these, and she wondered what else the newborns from the fourth trials might be capable of.

The toddlers from the first three series were all still being studied, so why Lab 4? As soon as she thought it, she knew. Of course, it would be unlucky number four. Had her work on Series 4 been the only differing factor? N-Gen hadn't hired her until the end of the second trials, and she'd only been allowed to observe the third.

Out of all the workers at N-Gen, the babies spared only her. Why? Male #4's intense gaze and how he'd studied her when she'd chastised the tech came to mind. Was that singular act of caring mistaken for mothering? She had to assume so. Perhaps they knew more, like her part in their creation. Confident in her work, she thought it impossible at first. But now . . . was all this her fault? What would happen when the babies figured out how there was a whole world outside N-Gen?

Their cries came.

This cycle of feedings then napping between questions and thoughts of dread and hopelessness had gone on for days. How many, Ting didn't know. Their schedule became hers.

After going through every plausible explanation in her mind, Ting concluded that something she'd done differently during the CRISPR process had altered the course of fetal development compared to the other trials. Therefore, she had to end it—these god-babies should not exist—but she needed a plan.

As she fed the newborns, they didn't show any awareness of her thoughts, but what would they do if they knew? They'd obviously developed powers of telekinesis and psychokinesis but so far showed no signs of precognition. So how could she get rid of them? All she knew was that she had to stop them.

Ting shambled down the hall toward the rotting corpses. Her extra hands made rifling through lab coats quicker. She'd found lint, paperclips, and various scraps of paper listing everything from specific nucleotides to recipes. Then she found a key. It seemed useless since the babies had sealed all the doors, but she turned the body over and saw "Dr. Cheng" embroidered on the front of the lab coat. He was also a surgeon and had access to the operating room. From time to time, the children from Labs 1–3 had to be anesthetized for scans and minor procedures.

Sluggish and barely able to keep her eyes open, Ting considered Dr. Cheng's key. The babies hadn't sealed the door to the operating room because no one had been in there at the time. She considered Dr. Samuelson's journal and his opioid studies. There had to be drugs stored in the room. Ting needed those anesthetic medications. All of them.

But first, they had to eat.

Many feedings had passed since she'd concocted her plan. Ting remembered scrambling away from the babies after the last time they ate. The ten of them wailed now in the nursery behind her, rattling the glass wall she'd slept against. Good. It meant that they still hadn't acquired or realized abilities for telepathy or precognition, didn't know she had rummaged through what remained of Lab 4's corpses for information from the doctors and scientists who'd designed them. That she had a plan to destroy them.

The extra sets of arms and stumpy pair of legs they'd attached to her bulk made her remarkably lithe. She stood in one smooth motion. After only three adjustments, the newborns configured the precise torso expansion necessary to accommodate all the limbs and breasts for the optimum feeding of ten. Ting felt both proud and horrified as she studied her reflection in the glass. All the eyes bothered her the most, but at least, she controlled where they looked and what they saw.

The doors parted, and she stepped into the nursery. Her hands went to work, gathering up the infants and cradling them, putting them to nipples. Ting rocked them as they suckled. Afterward, she changed their diapers, swaddled them, and put them back into their plastic bassinets. If she didn't leave, they'd cry until she picked them up again, so she exited the nursery and waited for their wailing to stop.

Sitting on the floor of the operating room, Ting wrapped IV tubing she'd found with flesh-colored adhesive and considered the time it might take for drugs to pass through her bloodstream, mammary glands, breastmilk, and into the infants. She was overthinking it. Her body had changed so much, it didn't matter, and she had no other options. Ting's biggest worry now was that the babies would become aware of the narcotics being pumped into her while they fed, so she did her best to camouflage it. If they caught on, they'd do something to her and all the planning and work would have been for nothing.

Ting concealed the small IV pump with the beige tape best she could. She'd practiced wrapping it around her body, tucking it under breasts and folds of skin. After emptying a 250-mL IV bag, she injected every anesthetic agent and narcotic she could find: fentanyl, hydromorphone, morphine, even the paralytic agent succinylcholine and the sedative-hypnotic propofol, which was white and why she had to conceal all the equipment in the first place. She'd heard Dr. Samuelson call it the milk of amnesia, and it was this memory that had set her plan into motion.

Ting set the pump to bolus and continuous flow, so even after she'd passed out and died, the medications would be delivered until the bag had emptied. She used the last of the three-inch tape to cover the IV bag and adhered it to her innermost thigh.

While tearing through another cabinet in the single operating room, Ting found bottles of oxycodone and codeine. If only she had a mouth to take them with. She considered crushing the tabs and snorting them but thought it would just be easier to insert them rectally. She busied a few of her hands with this task and continued camouflaging the IV tubing, medication pump, and bag full of death onto her body with another roll of the colored adhesive tape she'd located in a drawer.

From what she could see with her many eyes in the reflective steel cabinets, the job she did to mask the equipment worked.

Ting stood and went to the nursery. This would be the last time she'd feed the newborns.

She hoped that they'd gotten used to her dozing off during their feedings and wouldn't be alarmed this time either. Standing out in the hall, she stared at the babies through the glass. Seeming like innocent sleeping angels, no one would guess these infants were all-powerful gods. Isn't that why they look that way? To pull a mother's heart strings with angelic faces? But she was not their mother technically, and before she had too much time to think on it, Ting stepped quietly into the nursery as she always had and locked the door behind her, gently sliding a metal bar through the handles, trying not to alert the babies that anything was different. Her vision blurred, and the room tilted as she approached.

Male #4 opened his eyes, saw her, and began to cry. Then the others joined in as she lifted them up from their bassinets.

Ting put them to breasts, and they ate. After a minute, they stopped and cried, making sour faces as if they tasted something acrid. She readjusted and shifted the little bundles around her to different nipples until their hunger got the better of them.

Her body swayed, so she lowered herself to the floor without falling over and rocked the infants, humming a lullaby her own mother used to sing, to calm them further.

When Ting's eyes closed, she would jerk her body awake to keep the babies feeding. A smile of self-satisfaction crossed her face, but maybe the medications made her smile—or just knowing her plan would work.

The ground quaked with an explosion, jarring her as she drifted off again. Then another. On the other side of the nursery glass, looking in, were a few of the corpses she'd lined up against a far wall. They rammed their heads into the door, trying to break it open. Old blood and sloughed tissue left smears and streaks.

This had to be the newborns' way of getting help. They'd "resurrected" the dead to stop her. Maybe they'd developed telepathy after all. Or perhaps they knew her plans through her milk.

Ting rocked the babies, frantic yet listless. The metal bar shifted in the handles and clanged against the floor. Ting inched her way toward it to block the entryway. Three more of her dead colleagues had arrived, slapping the glass with their hands, leaving their skin stuck there. The first ones no longer had faces but continued striking their skulls into the nursery wall.

Ting stretched for the metal bar but couldn't reach. She adjusted the babies and tried again, her fingertips barely grazing it. The cold surge of medication pumped into her thigh as she struggled to reach the bar one last time. Her middle finger sent it rolling. She conceded and sat upright, refusing to look at her coworkers and friends.

As she drifted off, the babies also fluttered their eyelids. Ting adjusted them around her as she slumped to the side.

Multiple pings sounded against the glass. She saw rotted corpses on the floor now at eye level. Footfalls and . . . shouting sounded from the hall. Ting could no longer move. Her labored breathing grew shallower and stopped.

More gunfire came. A loud bang. Glass exploded. Men in boots and uniforms, soldiers, came through a wall.

"What the fuck is that?" one of them shouted.

They rushed toward her. Help had finally come.

You're too late, she thought.

They're Americans. How are they Americans? Where was she?

A soldier snatched one of the newborns from her. "It's alive!"

"Donovan, Jacobs, Reynolds, get those babies out of here. And tell medevac to go straight to the ship anchored off Yuerba Buena Island."

No, Ting thought. They must die.

With everything she had left, she reached for one of the babies.

"Look out," someone shouted.

"That thing's alive!"

"Was," said the lieutenant.

Ting felt nothing, but her head moved and her eyelids opened.

Male #4 stared back at her over a soldier's shoulder, a stronger sense of knowing in those tiny eyes.

§

Rena Mason is a horror and dark speculative fiction author and three-time Bram Stoker Award winner for *The Evolutionist* and "The Devil's Throat" as well as a 2014 Stage 32/The Blood List Search for New Blood quarter-finalist.

She is a member of the Horror Writers Association, Mystery Writers of America, International Thriller Writers, the International Screenwriters' Association, and the Public Safety Writers Association.

An avid scuba diver, she enjoys traveling the world and incorporating the experiences into her stories. She currently resides in Olympia, Washington. For more information, please visit her website at www.RenaMason.ink.

FLOAT DAY

S.B. Divya

I submitted my poem to the National Youth Poetry Contest yesterday, exactly two weeks after Float Day. Then I worked up the nerve to send it to Grace and Kelsey. I don't know if it'll be enough to make them start talking again, but if it doesn't, I swear I will find myself some new best friends. I am so sick of them fighting and using me as their messenger.

I almost wish Float Day had never happened.

I'm an only child. I sleep in on Saturdays, and nobody bothers me about it because I'm fifteen years old. Except for *that* day. *That* day, my mom shook me awake. I opened my eyes and saw her looming over me.

"Sneha," she sputtered. Her hands did some kind of dance at my body, then hers, and then the ground.

After I pushed myself upright, I realized my whole body was floating about three inches above my bed. It felt like I was lying in bed, and the cheap mattress sagged like it normally did, but my eyes told a different story.

Then I noticed that my mom's feet didn't quite touch the ground. She was freaked out. I thought it was pretty cool once I got over the weirdness of feeling things that weren't touching me. I guess it's harder for adults to deal with this kind of thing. We learned a bit about brains in biology and how kids have more plasticity than adults, so they're better at adapting to new stuff.

Anyway, I started experimenting with floating while my parents could not tear themselves away from their phones and the news. I texted Kelsey and Grace right after I got up. I didn't really care what happened to the world except for my family, my two best friends, and my cats. The cats were so hilarious. They kept swiping at the gap between my feet and the ground.

Me, Kelsey, and Grace have had a group text going since we became friends in seventh grade. We had three *years* of history. And stupid Float Day messed it up.

Kelsey sent a selfie of her butt hovering like six inches above her beanbag. Grace didn't reply, and we figured she was still asleep, but when noon rolled by without an answer, we got worried. I live closer, but Kelsey has a bike, so she rode over to Grace's house in East Lake Estates. That's when we discovered that Grace and her whole family were rooted. They had zero float.

Kelsey video-called me from outside Grace's house. Her pale skin had red blotches, and she looked like she was going to cry.

"Grace slammed the door in my face!" she sputtered. "She's not floating."

"At all?"

"Nope. Same with her parents."

"Weird," I said, half distracted by trying to see if I could use my float to skate down the staircase.

"Sneha! Pay attention! She shut me out. It was super mean. You have to text her and find out why."

I focused on my phone's screen and Kelsey's face and held back a sigh. I swear those two could act like a bickering couple instead of best friends. "Okay, I'll ask her what's up."

Kelsey hung up before I could laugh at my pun. I wondered how she looked while floating and riding her bike.

I texted Grace: *What's your damage?* We'd watched this old movie, *Heathers*, for movie night a few weeks before, and we loved saying that to each other any time it was even vaguely appropriate. I hoped the humor would get through to our friend.

Grace finally replied in our group chat: *Sorry, Kelsey! My parents think something's wrong with people who float, and they're freaking out. They don't want to be near anyone who's off the ground. They're worried it's contagious.*

Whatever, Kelsey replied. *You're old enough to rise above your parents' BS.*

Before I could ask if Kelsey's pun was intentional, Grace replied, *Easy for you to say. You're white. Your parents expect you to rebel. Back me up, Sneha!*

I had to admit that Grace was right. Her parents were from China and mine from India. I knew no good could come of me taking sides though, so I tried to be as diplomatic as I could.

It's true, I wrote. *But Grace, you could've said that to Kelsey's face instead of slamming the door on her.*

Grace replied with a "See, I'm right" GIF, and Kelsey sent an eye-rolling one.

That weekend, everyone shared their float heights and tried to figure out what it meant, how it happened, and why it worked. Scientists all over the world got into it. Nobody could explain the how or why, but pretty soon, people had figured out that you floated higher if you had less stuff. You didn't have to buy it yourself—otherwise all the babies would've floated away—but it had to belong to you. The actual cost of the stuff didn't seem to matter. Hoarders were rooted same as rich people. Someone from Tibet posted a video of laughing monks trapped against the ceiling of their monastery.

People could still interact with things. Other than the ground, everything worked like normal, including gravity, but it didn't hurt as much if you fell and had a high float. You could also run faster. The physicists explained something about friction, and some of the juniors from school made jokes about frictionless surfaces, but I didn't really get it.

Bottom line: float didn't seem to be contagious. Grace's parents refused to let her out of the house though. Kelsey and I went to the local playground and found it empty of the usual parents and grubby toddlers. We had fun playing with our newfound "floatabilities," and before long, other teenagers came out to join us. The people with higher float could do better tricks, like jumping off the tops of slides and landing without pain. I could feel the ground when I dropped, but the impact hurt, and I often ended up sliding onto my butt. Using the swings took a whole new set of skills.

The only adults who came outside were walking their dogs and talking furiously on their phones. Everyone we saw had at least some float.

On Sunday morning, my parents did the usual video call with my grandparents. They lived in Kochi, India, and all they could talk about was—of course—floating. My grandparents had a smaller house and way less stuff than we did, but they had a similar float. That posed a new puzzle, and pretty soon, they'd all switched to arguing about it in Malayalam, and I kind of faded from the conversation.

A bunch of kids from school had posted in our message group, mostly video clips of the random stuff they figured out how to do while floating. The skaters ate a lot of concrete, but the better ones started to figure out new tricks. I noticed that Grace and a few others remained silent, and I wondered if they all had zero float. I posted myself sliding down our staircase, including the one where I totally failed and crashed—and then posted it again in the thread with Kelsey and Grace. Kelsey applauded, but Grace said nothing. I felt bad that she couldn't join in the fun and annoyed that she couldn't get over herself.

Monday morning at school was weird. The kids with the nice cars and latest phones and best shoes had their feet planted solidly on the ground. The rest of us had fun checking each other out—including the teachers—but the rooted stayed quiet.

I elbowed Grace as we walked to biology. "So you don't float. So what? You're still my best friend."

"It's not fair," she protested. "It's not my fault that my parents bought me so much stuff."

"Give some of it away. I read this morning about people doing that, and it totally worked to increase their float."

"My parents are convinced this is all temporary, so they won't let me get rid of anything. I'm stuck like this!" Her voice quavered.

I put my arm around her shoulders for a gentle hug and let go as we entered class. Ms. Somers, our biology teacher, floated higher than any of us. We spent the entire period talking about whether float could affect our anatomy instead of our actual unit, the parts of a cell. I did my best to enjoy it and ignore the negative vibes coming off Grace like heat from an oven.

By Friday, a bunch of students had formed a local chapter of Do More with Less. They were organizing a drive to collect things that people didn't want anymore. The movement had worldwide support with many countries saying they would take essential items for their poorest. Turned out that float had a radius of effect, kind of like magnetism, so large sections of poor people had floats in proportion to their neighbors and the people they interacted with. That explained why the homeless in downtown Los Angeles had drifted up past the rooftops.

"You both should join," Kelsey said during lunch. "You don't have to help with the collection drive to be part of the group."

Grace shrugged. Her mood hadn't improved over the week.

"Come on, Grace," Kelsey prodded. "Haven't your parents gotten over this yet? Don't they want to float?"

"They're talking about moving," Grace said. "A more expensive neighborhood where we'd be in the middle and have some float."

I glanced at Kelsey. We had plans for senior prom that we'd hatched back in ninth grade. Our high school was one of the best in the state, and we figured we'd be together until graduation. If Grace moved, we wouldn't get to do any of that.

But Kelsey had a totally different expression on her face: rage.

"That is the grossest thing I've heard yet," she seethed. "Isn't it enough that rich people still have all the real power? Float doesn't make it easier to afford food or healthcare. Float doesn't pay for college or car insurance. You can't let the rest of us have one good thing in our lives to make up for everything else we have to deal with? Or are you one-percenters worried that we'll stop consuming so much crap and destroy your precious economy?"

Grace and I stared at Kelsey, our mouths hanging open. She'd always been more political than either of us, but we'd never heard her go off like that before.

"If you think you're so much better," Grace said through tight lips, "then why don't you go to Compton and try being one of the richest people around?"

Kelsey slammed a hand on the table. "Have I ever, in all of these years, said anything about your iPhone or your Beats or your Miu Miu backpack?"

"No, and I don't judge you for your H-and-M jeans!" Grace shot back.

"You guys," I interjected, "stop fighting! None of this matters, not your stuff or your float."

Two pairs of angry eyes turned toward me.

"You can't stay neutral forever, Sneha," Kelsey said. "You have to take a stand for something in life. Don't you think maybe this is the sign that society needs to change? We have a literal manifestation of everything that's wrong with capitalism."

"I . . . I don't know, Kelsey. I've never thought about it. Can't we go back to having fun with float instead of making it so serious?"

"Sure, do that," Grace said. Her tone dripped so much bitterness it could've been straight coffee. "Go back to having fun without me."

"It's not our fault that you're rooted," Kelsey shot back.

"Don't call me that word!"

Kelsey stabbed a finger at her. "If you had more guts, you would do something about it!"

I shook my head and went to throw away my trash. I knew exactly where this was going because we'd been down this road before. Five minutes later, Kelsey and Grace stopped speaking to each other. At least they had the weekend to cool off and make up.

Monday rolled around, and Kelsey and Grace still weren't on speaking terms.

I texted our little group between first and second period: *You guys, midterms next week. Are we studying together or what?*

Tell Grace to join Do More with Less, Kelsey wrote.

Tell Kelsey to apologize for using a floatist slur about me, Grace wrote.

K: OMG, it's not a slur!

G: Only because you think you're better than everyone.

S.T.O.P., I wrote.

A minute later, they'd deleted their messages.

Luckily I had AP English for second period without either of them. Why couldn't they let this go already? I did my best to focus, especially with midterms coming up, but I didn't participate in the discussion of *Wuthering Heights* as much as I normally would. My teacher, Mr. Ayala, stopped me after class.

"I'm sorry—" I began.

"Are you—" he said.

We both stopped, and he gave me a look like, "What were you about to apologize for?" I shook my head and waved for him to go on.

Mr. Ayala gave a little shrug and smiled. "I was going to ask if you're ready to submit a poem or two to the National Youth Poetry Contest. The deadline is a week from today. I thought you had some strong contenders during our Emily Dickinson unit last month."

"Oh, right," I said. I'd totally forgotten about the contest, what with all the float stuff and my best friends ready to kill each other. "I'll get you something by Friday."

"Great," he said. "I look forward to it."

Later, in biology class, we had to do a microscopy lab, and Grace kept whispering to me, trying to get me on her side about the word *rooted* and how unfair the whole float thing was. During math class, Kelsey kept passing me notes, telling me I had to make Grace see reason. At lunch, they refused to sit with each other, and I didn't want to take sides, so I ate alone.

It went on like that all week. I studied by myself. I did my homework solo in my room. I spoke to Grace at ballet and Kelsey during tennis, but our message group stayed quiet. The last thing on my screen was me yelling *STOP*.

The bigger school groups had fractured as well. Three social clumps had formed: the zero-floaters, the Do More with Less people, and those of us who preferred to stay away from the serious stuff. I kept myself in the third group, but I couldn't laugh with them at the other two groups.

Fridays were movie nights, and we'd already missed one because of Grace and Kelsey's fight. I wanted us together again, laughing at cats or stupid dance moves, playing video games in Grace's basement, making microwave nachos at midnight when the rest of the world is asleep. Not giving each other the silent treatment and leaving me stuck in the middle.

They'd never gone for more than a week without talking. I didn't know how I could make them remember that they liked each other, that their float and their stuff—or lack of it—didn't have to change our friendship. We had two and a half years before college ripped us apart for good, maybe less if Grace's parents actually moved. How could they let Float Day spoil our time together?

On Thursday, I remembered about the poetry contest and opened up my files from the Dickinson unit. I'd written a poem about the pain and thrill of toe shoes and another about women in Kochi tending rice paddies. They both seemed trite. Insipid. Banal. Deeply unworthy of winning a poetry contest after Float Day.

I opened a blank document and stared at the screen.

Then I typed my pent-up anger and sadness and love, all in a rush.

I reached the last word and read it from top to bottom, changing little. I shrugged, closed the file, and sent it to Mr. Ayala. In the grand scheme of my life at that moment, I couldn't care about a poetry contest enough to try any harder. With shaky fingers, I pasted my words into our message group. Sometimes you have to go all in on the gamble.

It's Friday morning, and I'm floating above my bed. The poster of a cat from the *Warriors* series still hangs in my view. I haven't read those books in years. Why do I still have that poster on my wall? I'm trying very hard not to reach for my phone. I'd put it in airplane mode after I sent my poem. I knew I wouldn't sleep otherwise, and even then, it took me a while to wind down.

I decide I'll get ready for school without looking, so I carry my phone face down and slip it into my backpack. My mom arches an eyebrow at me for reading a book rather than being on my tablet over breakfast.

"Who's hosting movie night?" she asks.

I wish I could pretend like I didn't hear her. "I don't know," I mutter.

She makes a sympathetic noise. "Oh no, are Kelsey and Grace still fighting? I'm sorry. I'm sure they'll make up in time. You never miss movie night."

"No kidding? Like how we didn't miss it last Friday?"

"Don't take your hard feelings out on me," she scolds.

Out of the corner of my eye, I see her slip a Hershey's Kiss into my lunch bag, but it's not going to cheer me up if the worst happens. As she drives me to school, I finally take my phone out of airplane mode and check my messages. The last few lines of my poem sit at the bottom of my message thread with Grace and Kelsey.

Stuck
in the middle
I
didn't know
how to bridge their gap

So I wrote this poem
to say
forget
the rest of the world

Forget
your float
and
your stuff
and
your ambitions

because
we can have
each other

and
love
weighs
nothing

I reach the end. There's an email from Mr. Ayala who thinks it's great. The school thread has forty-eight new messages. I ignore them and go back to my best friend group chat. The screen stays blank-white after my poem.

My finger's over the power button when a bubble appears in green.

I vote Sneha's house for tonight. From Grace.

Then another bubble in purple.

Works for me. Wonder Woman 2?

§

S.B. Divya is a lover of science, math, fiction, and the Oxford comma. She enjoys subverting expectations and breaking stereotypes whenever she can. Divya is the Hugo and Nebula nominated author of *Machinehood* (Saga), *Runtime* (tordotcom), and the short story collection *Contingency Plans for the Apocalypse and Other Situations* (Hachette India). She co-edits the weekly science fiction podcast *Escape Pod* with Mur Lafferty. Her short stories have been published at various magazines such as *Analog*, *Uncanny*, and tor.com as well as in anthologies including *The Gollancz Book of South Asian Science Fiction* and *Where the Stars Rise*. She holds degrees in computational neuroscience and signal processing, and she worked for twenty years as an electrical engineer before becoming an author. Find out more about her at www.sbdivya.com or on Twitter as @divyastweets.

THE MYSTERY WATCH

Gerald L. Coleman

"The concept behind Mystery clocks and watches is to hide the mechanics from view, creating a 'mystery' of functionality."

—Meehna Goldsmith

"One ever feels his twoness—an American, a Negro; two souls, two thoughts, two unreconciled strivings; two warring ideals in one dark body, whose strength alone keeps it from being torn asunder."

—W.E.B. DuBois, *The Souls of Black Folk*

L exington in the fall was El's favorite. The leaves were a lovely jumble of yellow, orange, green, and red. The temperature was a dopamine-inducing seventy degrees. He had been thankful for the balmy temperature when the cop slammed his face into the hood of his car. His crime had been driving a 1964 Aston Martin DB5 while black—and an acerbic witticism concerning whether the cop had time to harass him and get to Dunkin Donuts before all the jelly-filled were gone. El sat on the curb in handcuffs. His heart beat wildly in his chest, like the hooves of the thoroughbreds at Keeneland, while the cop ran his registration. His hands weren't shaking because there was anything for the cop to find. They were shaking because he was black. And this is America.

Nothing said Lexington quite like the seven cruisers that showed up for an innocuous traffic stop. El's window-paned, navy-blue, three-piece Tom Ford suit and his impeccable manners hadn't mattered. They never did. What mattered was the cop's high-school education, the trailer-park-sized chip on his shoulder, and a certain kind of ineluctable bias that came with seeing El's expensive wingtips. El sat there, outwardly calm like his mother taught him when he was seven. He knew the game. It did not stop his running commentary on everything from officer Cavanaugh's flop sweat to his heavy breathing. If he had to sit there, he might as well do something with his time.

Cavanaugh came back frowning. "Well, Mr. Elwood Spaulding"—he squinted at El's license—"you're free to go."

He stood El up, removed the cuffs, and handed him his license and registration.

As he walked off, he called over his shoulder, "You drive safely now, you hear."

El couldn't resist as he rubbed at his wrists. "Mad you didn't find anything, huh? I got your badge number, Cavanaugh. Pick me up a cruller, will you?"

The cop stopped for a brief moment and stiffened but kept walking. It was all he could do. El learned early on not to ride *dirty*. You never give them any ammunition they could use against you. An expired tag could get you killed. He took satisfaction from the fact that the cop would sulk all day. It was satisfaction the size of a grain of rice but satisfaction nonetheless. El took a long, deep breath and let it out slowly. And then he took another one. There was a reason black men died from heart disease and high blood pressure. And it wasn't all from a bad diet or hereditary predispositions.

As El walked slowly back to his car, he noticed two black women with their cellphones aimed at him as white folks passed behind them on the sidewalk without so much as a sideways glance. He smiled at them, gave them the nod, and held his hand, palm up, in their direction. They returned the gesture. El could almost hear the unspoken, *We got you.*

When he slid back into the black leather seat of his car, he rested his hands on the wooden steering wheel. The shakes had subsided to a mild tremor. He sent a quick text before turning the key and hearing the roar of the pristinely restored engine as he revved it. He opened his music, cued up a song, and turned up the volume, the FM transmitter sending the signal from his cellphone to his classic radio. El smiled at the cops milling about by their cruisers as he slowly pulled off.

His speakers boomed, "Fuck the police comin' straight from the underground! A young nigga got it bad 'cause I'm brown . . ."

El waited a few blocks before he turned the volume down to a respectable level and switched the song from NWA to Digable Planets. He fast-forwarded until he reached Ladybug Mecca, the only woman of the three, rapping the chorus, "I'm chill like that, I'm chill like that, I'm chill like that, I'm chill like that, I'm chill like that, I'm chill like that, I'm chill like that, I'm chill." He leaned back in the seat, letting the jazz-style thrumming of the upright bass slow his heartbeat and unclench his teeth. His head started to bob unconsciously to the beat.

It was early afternoon on a Friday, and he was just pulling into town. Twenty years had passed since he'd been home for more than a few days at a time. Kentucky in general, and Lexington in particular, hadn't changed much. The city's layout was a little different, here and there, but not the people. Spalding's Bakery, the purveyors of the best glazed donuts on the planet, had moved from Third Street to Winchester. He hadn't been there yet, so he didn't know if they had taken the bell over the door with them. The jangling sound it made when you walked in made your mouth water. It was downright Pavlovian.

Whole sections of the city had been gentrified. Rose Street, which ran the width of the University of Kentucky's campus, was permanently closed to traffic. It was once a quick thoroughfare that would connect you to Limestone, headed toward south campus, the hospital, and the mall. Now it was a plush walkway lined with flowerbeds and manicured shrubbery. North Park was gone. El had seen Flash Gordon and Eddie Murphy's comedy specials at the movie theater that once occupied that strip mall. He had immediately regretted trying to watch *Raw* there. The audience was so loud he couldn't hear half the jokes. Even Tolly-Ho—it was a college rite of passage to eat a Ho burger at one in the morning on a Friday night after stumbling across the street from the student center—had moved.

But Lexington still smelled the same. Instead of coming in on I-75, a straight shot from Atlanta, El passed through Chattanooga, Nashville, and made his way onto treelined Bluegrass Parkway. It was his favorite way of driving into his hometown. When he exited onto Versailles, he always rolled down his window and took a deep breath. It was like he could smell the horse farms and casual racism. It still made him smile. It was home.

El didn't have to be on campus to give his first philosophy lecture until next Wednesday. He reserved the weekend to move into his house and reacclimate to the city. Being pulled over ten minutes after getting to town was a start, even if an unwelcome one. He was still looking forward to a dozen glazed donuts and a plate of Hoppin' John at Alfalfa's. But first, he needed to get the keys to his new place. The movers were scheduled to arrive in a few hours.

A quick turn onto Main Street took him through downtown, past Triangle Park with its full-length fountain and Rupp Arena on his left and shops on his right. There had been slave jails where some of those shops were. Lexington was born on the backs of enslaved Africans. In 1860, a little under half the population of the city was enslaved. The city underwent a massive facelift in the early eighties when they bid on hosting the NCAA's Sweet Sixteen. In order to win, they were forced to add parks and accommodations. While they were doing that, they also cleaned up some of the remnants of the city's dark history.

El turned right onto Jefferson, passing Harrison Magnet School on his right. When it was his elementary, it had simply been Harrison. Another four blocks and he turned right onto Fourth. Halfway down Fourth, he glanced to his left and took a quick look at the small apartment complex where he had lived up until sixth grade. It looked so small. He crossed North Broadway, passing Transylvania University's main campus on the right, and turned right onto North Upper. Another quick right put him on West Third, and a left brought him to North Mill Street and Gratz Park. Halfway down the block, just before reaching the Carnegie Center, he pulled into the driveway of his new home. It was a lovely little neighborhood made up of expensive houses on narrow, tree-lined streets. El turned off his car and got out. Margo Underwood was waiting for him on the porch with a set of keys.

The porch was three stone steps up from the front yard, covered, and ran half the width of the red, brick house. The small front yard was perfectly manicured with a black wrought-iron fence around it. When El stepped onto the porch, he was greeted with a bright smile. Margo Underwood was small, plump, and dark-brown. Her hair was long, thick, and sprung up off her head and down to her shoulders like a park fountain. She was wearing a smart, navy-blue, pinstriped suit and black heels. She smelled like honeysuckle. Her handshake was firm. Her voice was soft.

"Good afternoon, Mr. Spaulding. I hope your drive up was nice."

El smiled down at the small woman and replied, "Yes, it was pleasant—for the most part. Thank you for meeting me here with the keys. I hope I didn't keep you waiting long?"

Underwood shook her head and said, "Oh, it was no problem. I love Gratz Park. I just sat on the steps at the Carnegie Center and enjoyed the weather until I got your text."

She handed El the keys and said, "I don't usually pry, but may I ask you something?"

She was holding her head at a slight angle and softly biting her lower lip.

Curious, El said, "Sure. Ask away."

Underwood grinned and leaned forward just a bit. "In all the years I've been selling properties, I've never seen someone go through or put up with the amount of vetting that you have. I was shocked at what the former owner was asking for. I actually thought I was going to lose the sale. I heard he even hired a private investigator to check into your background, your politics, and your family. Do you have any idea why?"

El smiled and chuckled softly. "Ms. Underwood, I have absolutely no clue. I chalked it up to eccentricity. I only put up with it because I love the location. Having Gratz park right out my front door was a big incentive. And I like invading this small enclave of white privilege. The former owner has a quiet but honored reputation in our community, so I indulged him. I can only imagine what he's lived through in eighty years as a black man in Lexington."

Underwood nodded and said, "Mmmhmm. I know exactly what you mean."

She went on to ask if he'd like her to walk him through the house, but he decided he would rather experience it for himself. El had seen all the pictures of the interior, but it was nothing like actually seeing a place with your own eyes. She handed him the keys with a smile and excused herself.

El opened the front door and entered. The faint smell of bleach and something citrusy greeted him. It was a large house with high ceilings and big windows. The first floor was what you'd expect. There was a small foyer with archways to the right and left leading to the front rooms. A hallway straight ahead, leading back to a bathroom, dining room, and kitchen, was bordered on the left by the staircase leading to the second and third floor. El headed upstairs.

The second floor contained three bedrooms, two bathrooms, and a sunroom. After a quick circuit, he headed up to the third floor. It was the third floor that had convinced him to buy. It had been remodeled into a single, massive bedroom with a sitting area, a small dinette, and a desk for work. There was an extremely large walk-in closet with an island and a bathroom with a glass-encased shower, a glorious, modern, glossy wood bathtub that looked like the side of sailboat, and enough room to take a small stroll. Oddly, there was a white door opposite the entrance to the bathroom. He didn't remember seeing that in the pictures.

Not one to leave an oddity unexplored, El opened the door. To his surprise, it was another walk-in closet. He turned on the light and saw a small island in the middle, plain walls without actual bars to hang clothes, a standing mirror covered in a long sheet, and an oversized leather chair. His shoes clacked softly on the hardwood floor as he crossed to the island. Sitting in the middle of the island was a small, blue leather box with a small manila envelope next to it. El picked up the envelope and opened it. Inside was a small, manila card. It said, *Enjoy.* That was it. It wasn't signed.

El put down the card and opened the leather box. Inside was a magnificent pocket watch. Immediately he could tell it was old. It was silver or white gold—or maybe platinum? The bow over the latch release was larger than normal. He pushed the release and opened the case. It was breathtaking. The edge of the face was covered by an inch-wide band of embellishment surrounding the dial with the numbers and the hands. Diamonds were encrusted around the outside edge. The truly wonderous part was the interior area where the hour and minute hands were. It was perfectly clear. The hands looked as if they were floating in mid-air. El could not see a single movement or watch complication. It had a double Albert chain made of whatever silver-colored metal the watch was made from. It was also encrusted with tiny, sparkling diamonds.

El just stood there holding it. Elias John Jackson Toussaint was a quiet and eccentric, elderly black man. El only knew him by reputation. It was said he loved the black community and was always there to support it, though he liked to work in the background, out of the spotlight. He was instrumental in helping the cause during the civil rights movement, though no one really talked about exactly what he did. He had money and a clear point of view about how to use it. But he hadn't ever been ostentatious. In a lot of ways, he reminded El of his grandfather—but without the money. Had the old man left the pocket watch as a gift? It looked like it was worth as much as the house.

El pulled out his phone and googled pocket watches with invisible complications. It took a minute, but he found out what it was. It was called a mystery watch, which according to Wikipedia was a watch *whose working is not easily deducible because it seems to have no movement at all or the hands do not seem to be connected to any movement.* El had no idea that was even a thing.

He closed the case, slid the watch into his vest pocket, and fixed the chain across his vest, sliding the T-bar through a buttonhole and putting the fob in the other pocket. The double Albert was meant to hang across the front of a vest like a *W.* A small bit of change hung from the T-bar in the center of the chain. On its end was a small, diamond-encrusted medallion. El almost missed that it had an anvil engraved on its face.

With the pocket watch in place, El left the odd little closet, turned off the light, and closed the white door. By the time he made his way back downstairs, the movers were knocking. El grimaced. The white men he'd hired were a handful. They reminded him of that quote from Lyndon B. Johnson about convincing the lowest white man that he's better than the best colored man. They had acted like they were doing him a favor taking his money to move him. If he hadn't discovered that attitude at the last minute, he would've fired them. As it was, it took all his patience. He had made it abundantly clear that he'd sue them to within an inch of their financial lives if they damaged his things. Some of it was irreplaceable, like the antiques that had been in his family for generations.

El took a deep breath and opened the door. He was determined that he wasn't going to let them ruin his homecoming. The supervisor was standing there holding a clipboard with a sour look on his face.

Before he could even open his mouth, El launched into the void. "Listen, I don't care what your disposition is. If you want to be paid, you will unload this furniture according to the labels, and you'll do it without a single word. Do you understand me? Because, so help me god, if I have to correct a single attitude, there'll be hell to pay. Do you understand me?"

The man stood there in shock for a moment before snatching his cap off his head and stuttering, "M-My apologies, sir. I had no idea. I'm very sorry. It's just that—"

El cut him off saying, "Nope. No. I don't want to hear it. Just get to work."

The man ducked his head in a weird half-bow, slapped his cap back on his head, turned, and began bellowing orders. It was like night and day. In Atlanta, El had to constantly look over their shoulders and berate them to pick up the pace. That was unnecessary here in Lexington. They moved quickly but carefully. Each man ducked past El like he was going to strike them at any moment. He watched in amazement as their condescension became humility. As he watched, something the supervisor said started to nag at him. What did the man mean by, "I had no idea"? No idea about what? That El wasn't going to put up with their shit anymore?

He watched as over the course of a few hours the men moved him into the new house, putting everything where it was supposed to go with efficiency and care. By the time the sun was going down, they were sweeping up behind themselves and tipping their caps as they passed him on their way out. It was odd, but El was too tired to think about it anymore. He was just glad his things were where they were supposed to be, and the white men were gone. He closed the door behind them and went to the kitchen. His study wasn't set up yet, so he grabbed a bottle of bourbon from one of the boxes in the kitchen and rummaged through the other boxes until he found a heavy, crystal whiskey glass.

He made his way out onto the porch and sat in one of the chairs he'd purchased in Atlanta for the purpose. Darkness was falling on Gratz Park. The lights in the Carnegie Center to his right flickered on, and he could see the lights in one of the buildings on the edge of Transylvania's campus down to his left. The round streetlamps that peppered the landscape in the park were glowing to life. El poured a couple of fingers of bourbon into the heavy glass and sat the bottle on the porch next to his chair. He pulled a cigar out of his suit jacket's inner pocket and retrieved his cutter and lighter from another pocket, and in a matter of moments, he was blowing heavy cigar smoke into the evening air and sipping on bourbon.

For the first time all day, he was able to relax. He sat there for a few hours, smoking, drinking, and enjoying the evening. A few of his neighbors passed by as they walked through the neighborhood. El didn't expect much from them given that he was invading their little white preserve. But to his surprise, they smiled and waved at him as they went by. El just smiled to himself and enjoyed the rest of his evening.

When he reached the end of his cigar, he headed back in the house. It had been a long day, so he found his sheets, blankets, and pillows, made up his bed, and crashed. He slept the sleep of the dead.

When his eyes slowly blinked open, he reached for his phone on the bedside table and checked the time. It was almost ten in the morning. He smiled at the amount of sleep he'd gotten. He rolled out of bed, hit the shower, and got dressed. It was Saturday, so he threw on jeans, a T-shirt, and grabbed his Chuck Taylors. He was hungry and didn't feel like cooking, so he decided to go out for breakfast. A couple was walking by when stepped out the front door and made his way to his car.

The man stopped by his driveway and said, "Hey, uh, are you the new owner?"

El said, "Yes, I am."

The guy looked like he might have gone to Sayre. It was the khaki pants and black penny loafers. He looked at the Aston Martin and back at El with raised eyebrows and said, "Is that your car?"

El opened the car door and said, "Yes, it is."

Sayre looked like he had sour milk in his mouth. He grabbed the woman's arm and dragged her down the sidewalk. He stopped a few feet away and watched El get in the car, start it up, and pull out of the driveway. El stopped the car over the sidewalk and gave the man his fakest smile. Sayre turned around and walked on down the sidewalk, pulling the woman along with him, as his loafers made a slapping sound on the concrete. El shook his head, pulled out into the street, and drove off. The more things changed, the more they stayed the same.

He drove down North Mill to Vine and turned left. He tried not to think about the difference in the waves and smiles from the night before and the disdain this morning. White folks were like that. You got used to it.

Main was a one-way street, so he had to drive up past where Alfalfa's was located before he could turn onto Main and make his way down to the restaurant. By some miracle, there was an open parking spot right out front. He parked and used his credit card to pay the meter. People stopped on the sidewalk to ogle the car. It was just something he had gotten used to.

One guy came over to him with a look of surprise on his face and said, "Is this your car?"

This was the other thing El had gotten used to. It wasn't the question that bothered him. He usually enjoyed talking about his car, and a fully restored classic Aston Martin drew attention. It was the occasional white guy whose tone said, *This couldn't be your car.*

The guy continued with a feigned chuckle, "What'd you do, steal it?"

El raised his American Express black card in a slow, exaggerated motion and slid it back in his wallet. He dead-faced the guy as he slid his wallet in his pocket and silently brushed past and went inside Alfalfa's. He took a deep breath and rolled his head around on his shoulders to release the tension as he waited for the host or hostess to return to their station to seat him. *Let it go, El,* he thought to himself. At least the Hoppin' John didn't disappoint.

El was back in his car in an hour and a half. Part of him wanted to drive around the city, but he decided to go back home. He spent the day unpacking and putting things into place. Before he knew it, night had come again. He showered and changed into a navy polo, jeans, and dress boots. He'd heard about a new place called Creaux in the city, and he was hungry again. He decided to grab the pocket watch on his way out. He put it in his front pocket and hooked the chain onto his beltloop, so it would be inconspicuous. Lexington wasn't a large city, and his new house was very close to downtown, so it didn't take long for him to get to Creaux. This time, he had to park around the corner and walk the half block to the restaurant.

As he turned the corner, he saw the same cop from yesterday hassling a young black guy on the sidewalk. Something in El flipped like a switch. Before he could think it through, he was in the cop's face, yelling. A lifetime of anger spilled out of him. He poured all the resentment about social injustice, abuse of power, and racial bigotry on the cop's head like an erupting volcano. El added a list of citizen's rights to his flaming denunciation of the cop's behavior. When he finally stopped, he realized the cop had steadily backed away from him as he poked him in his chest, punctuating every objection and grievance with a stiff finger. For some reason, Cavanaugh was still calmly asking him to understand that he was "only trying to do his job." El froze.

Why wasn't he on the ground with the cop's knee in his back? Why didn't he have a gun trained on him? Why was officer Cavanaugh being so polite, so solicitous? El's mouth must have been silently agape because the cop took it as an opportunity to extricate himself from the situation. As El stood there frozen to the sidewalk in shock, Cavanaugh raised his voice and told everyone to go on about their business, including the young black guy he had been harassing. He looked at El one more time and slowly made his way to his cruiser, adjusting his gun belt and scowling at everyone except El. The sound of the cruiser door slamming shut and the car pulling off with that two-note siren blip snapped El out of his shocked stupor. What the fuck had just happened?

Someone slapped his shoulder. El turned around to see the young black guy. He said, "Thank you, sir. I really appreciate it when someone like you steps in to help. I don't know what would've happened if you hadn't been here. I just wanted to say thank you."

El smiled and nodded. They shook hands, and El said, "No problem. Don't even worry about it. I got you, fam."

The young guy chuckled and said, "Oh, it's like that? Then I appreciate it, fam."

He added an odd emphasis on the word *fam*. But El ignored it. Sometimes younger folks found slang from someone his age humorous. He just stood there and watched the young guy go into Creaux and meet his friends who must have been watching from the front windows of the restaurant. They looked out at El as the young man pointed to him and spoke. They nodded and smiled. One young woman waved at El, and he waved back. She smiled and threw up a fist. El chuckled and repeated the gesture. She giggled and turned back to her small coterie of hip youngsters. El realized he had lost his appetite.

He went back to his car and drove home. He kept going back over the incident again and again in his mind. Why wasn't he in jail right now? Or dead? It was the look on the cop's face that puzzled him the most. It was—El fished for the exact word. It was *deferential.*

El parked his car and went into the house like he was on autopilot. He made his way upstairs and sat on the edge of his bed. He hadn't been sitting for more than a few seconds when he realized he needed a drink and a good chair to do the drinking in. He went back downstairs and grabbed some bourbon and a glass. He was about to sit in one of the chairs in the front room when he realized that the perfect chair was upstairs.

He went back to the odd closet, behind the white door in the bathroom, with the plush leather chair. When he sat down, it was like the cushioned leather reached out and hugged him. What a great chair. He poured some bourbon and sat there sipping. All the while, he was trying to figure out what had changed between Friday and Saturday that made the cop react so differently. It puzzled him, and he just sat there drinking.

After a while, El decided he wanted to finish his drinking on the porch. When he stood up, he realized that the only thing in the closet he hadn't really looked at was the mirror. It was still covered in a long white sheet. Maybe it was an antique. If it was nice and the right shade of wood, he could put it in the bedroom.

El grabbed a handful of sheet. With a flick of his wrist, he pulled on it and watched it slide away to the floor. He nearly dropped the glass in his hand.

"Holy shit."

El stared at his reflection in disbelief. *It must be a trick,* he thought. He walked into the bathroom and looked in the mirror over the sink. It was just his normal face. He went back into the strange closet and stood in the front of the mirror again.

"No fucking way."

El ran his hand through the blond hair reflected in the mirror. He leaned in close to see the blue eyes and thin pink lips. The thin nose and white skin was all a shock. He was a middle-aged white man.

"How the fuck is this happening?" And then he remembered the pocket watch.

El took the watch out of his pocket and laid it on the island. Then he turned back around and looked in the mirror. It was him—dark-brown skin, full lips, shaved head. It was still him. But when he put the pocket watch on, he looked like a white man. It was crazy.

He must have put it on and took it off a dozen times, and each time his reflection in the mirror changed—but only in this mirror. He ran up and down the stairs going to each bathroom in the house. Everywhere else, he looked like himself.

He walked back into the closet and stood in front of the antique mirror. It all suddenly made sense.

He stared into the mirror and muttered, "Holy shit."

And then he smiled.

§

Gerald L. Coleman is a philosopher, theologian, poet, and science fiction & fantasy author. He did his undergraduate work in philosophy, english, and religious studies, followed by a master's degree in theology. He is the author of the epic fantasy novel saga *The Three Gifts*, which currently includes *When Night Falls* (Book One), *A Plague of Shadows* (Book Two), and the upcoming *When Chaos Reigns* (Book Three), which is scheduled for release in 2021. His most recent poetry appears in *Pluck! The Journal of Affrilachian Arts & Culture*, *Drawn to Marvel: Poems from the Comic Books*, *Pine Mountain Sand & Gravel* (vol. 18), *Black Bone*, the 10th-anniversary issue of *Diode Poetry Journal*, *About Place Journal*, and *Star*line* (vol. 43, issue 4). His speculative fiction short stories appear in the science fiction cyberfunk anthology *The City*, *Rococoa* (by Roaring Lion), the urban fantasy anthology *Terminus*, the 2019 JordanCon anthology *You Want Stories?*, *Dark Universe: Bright Empire*, and *Cyberfunk!* (by MVMedia). He has been a guest author at DragonCon, Boskone, Blacktasticon, JordanCon, Atlanta Science Fiction & Fantasy Expo, The Outer Dark Symposium, World Horror Con, Imaginarium, and Multiverse. He served as a programme content consultant for WorldCon Dublin and the director of the fantasy track for MultiverseCon. He is a Rhysling Award nominee for 2021, a Scholastic National Writing juror, and a co-founder of the Affrilachian Poets. He has released four collections of poetry entitled *the road is long, falling to earth, microphone check*, and *Nappy Metaphysic*. You can find him at GeraldLColeman.com.

WAKE

Mary Anne Mohanraj

Amudhini reached out to touch her husband's hand, feeling guilty about disturbing his sleep but needing the reassurance. Outside their window, the sun was climbing in the sky, and all seemed well, but Amu's sleep had been troubled. A roiling mass of incoherent dreams, dark figures striding across a shadowed landscape, torches blazing. Stephen made a small, grumbly noise, but then his fingers curled around hers, squeezing.

"You okay?" he asked.

"Bad dreams."

He tugged, and she shifted closer, into the shelter of his arms. She pressed her face against his smooth chest, inhaled the reassuring scent of him. "Me too," he said. "All those torches . . ."

Amudhini took a quick, startled breath. It had been a long, long time since they'd walked in each other's dreams. It happened so rarely once the children had arrived. She'd assumed the gift had mostly been smothered by the daily weight of meal planning, homework supervising, doctor's appointments, and clothes sorting. Their minds were so full between the children and their own work that there wasn't much room left for . . . well, whatever the dreamwalking had been. They'd never really found a good word for it.

"Mom!" Roshan was at the bedroom door, sounding vaguely irritated. "Your phone keeps buzzing and buzzing." He held it out in one hand, his eyes still fixed on the device in his other hand, undoubtedly deep into whatever game he was currently playing.

"Thanks, sweetie." She'd decided to try keeping the phone *not* in the bedroom, hoping to sleep better, but hadn't factored in that some callers could be persistent. "It's Shruthi. I'd better call her back."

"You don't want to talk about this?" Stephen frowned in concern.

"Later," Amudhini said. She reluctantly left the shelter of his arms, sitting up in the bed. "Shruthi was on call last night, and you know Darnell is slammed right now too. She can't talk to him as much as she'd like. All the riots are bringing back bad memories from that time she got caught in one back in Sri Lanka. I'm sure she got a lot less sleep than we did."

Stephen nodded and settled back under the covers, closing his eyes—he was an owl, not a lark, and would be deep in sleep again shortly. Amudhini swung her legs out of the bed and got to her feet. Time to get to work.

The phone buzzed again a few minutes after she finished the call with Shruthi. A group text: *We'll be at the Cicero-290 bridge tonight, starting at 5. They're shutting down the subway. If you're walking over, don't walk alone. Join us if you can.*

The sewing machine hummed along soothingly—until it didn't—and Amudhini bit back a curse as it juddered to a halt. What now? She'd made hundreds of masks at this point, had gotten the rhythm down of turning the corners, avoiding getting fabric caught up as she backstitched, only needing to pause long enough to wind a new bobbin once in a while. If the machine cooperated, she could turn out four masks in an hour and usually could find an hour or two each day to sew in between work and the kids. But sometimes, it seemed like the machine was possessed by some demon, and there was nothing to do but summon every ounce of patience and try to diagnose the problem.

Patience had never been one of her virtues. She wanted it all, she wanted it badly, and she wanted it now.

But at almost-fifty, Amudhini had had a few lessons ground into her. She was slow as she tugged at the fabric, pulling it away enough to snip the thread tangle free. She was careful undoing the screws, removing the throat plate, opening up the dark heart of her willful monster. Nothing obvious, but she blew out a few forceful breaths, hoping to free whatever dust or bits of thread might be clogging the mechanism. And then put it all back together, rethreaded bobbin and spool once again, inserted the fabric, sent a little prayer out into the universe. *Please.* And then foot down, steady and slow—*Thank you, Universe.* It was working again.

Stephen's voice interrupted her moment of triumph and relief. "Are you going to help Roshan with his schoolwork? He's barely done any in a month, the teachers want *something* to assess before the end of the year, and I have to be on a Zoom from ten to twelve."

"Can you get him started? I'll try to check in." It had turned out that helping Roshan with schoolwork required every bit of patience that Amudhini had—and more. Mostly, she didn't even try, leaving it to Stephen, who didn't love it either but handled it better. "I promised Shruthi that I'd get her a dozen more masks for her nurses by the weekend. They're having a hard time breathing through the new yellow ones they've been issued."

"Okay," Stephen said. A little irritation in his voice but smothered down, and Amudhini wasn't worried about it. Mostly. He supported her sewing masks; he even cut the filter fabric for her to save her a little time. But he'd also asked, "Are you sure you need to be the one doing this? Is this the best use of your time?"

She didn't know. Amudhini didn't know what was the best use of her time, so she tried to do a little of everything. At least everything that she was good at, hoping that somewhere in there, she was doing some good. The world was so broken, especially now. Her friend Shmuel had told her there was a Jewish concept of tikkun olam, "repairing the world." He'd repeated the words one rabbi had supposedly said: *Do not be daunted by the enormity of the world's grief. You are not obligated to complete the work, but neither are you free to abandon it.*

Amudhini wasn't actually religious; she wasn't sure a god existed at all. But whatever she believed in, she believed in what they owed to each other as human beings. *You are not free to abandon it.*

Thread snapped. Dammit. Time to re-thread the machine. Again.

The last time she and Stephen had shared a dream was three years ago. They'd actually gone away for an anniversary, renting a room at the Drake for two nights, leaving the children with sitters. Meena thought that at ten she was definitely old enough to babysit eight-year-old Roshan, but her parents didn't agree. Amudhini hadn't quite known what to do with Stephen once she had him to herself—they'd eaten a nice meal, gone to a movie. The second day, they'd tried playing a board game, which went well enough, and they'd finally ended up in bed in the middle of the afternoon, enjoying slow, teasing sex, the kind of sex they hadn't had in years.

In the dream afterward, she was a lizard again, the way she'd been all those years before. It wasn't the avatar she would have chosen. Amudhini would've liked to be a lion or an elephant, something with substance. But no, a lizard sunning herself by the side of a pond. And Stephen a turtle, swimming placidly from side to side, thinking deep turtle thoughts. Nothing of consequence in the dream, but when they woke, he turned to her and smiled, and they were twenty-two again, when all of this had started. They'd had an entire summer living half in dream, and even now, Amudhini couldn't say quite why it had all unraveled.

But oh, that hurt to think about, and besides, there was more work to do. There was always more work to do.

The mom groups were full of anxiety, pandemic fears now overlaid with the rising tide of protests, violence erupting. Everyone talking, analyzing—are they really agitators rather than protestors, attacking cop cars, breaking store windows? They'd all been wound so tight after months of sudden shelter-in-place, so many losing jobs, losing homes, afraid of losing everything. It didn't seem surprising to her that the desperate might take an opportunity to take something back from an uncaring city.

Stephen thought the looters were actually agitators, but Amudhini wasn't so sure. He'd never had to scramble for a job, never dodged a landlord in a street the way she had, months behind on the rent. He didn't understand how terror gripped you, turning your stomach inside out as you stared at the bills, shunting money from one credit card to another, numbers just growing every time, threatening to eat you alive.

They'd argued last night before bed. Analysis was one of Stephen's strengths, and maybe this white man had a better handle on the situation than she did. She hoped he was right. But as she scrolled through the posts online, she couldn't help noticing how different the tone was between her Black friends and the rest. What was there that she didn't understand either? Brown wasn't the same as Black, even if they chose to stand shoulder to shoulder. Not in America.

In the progressive voter group, Shruthi had posted again and again. A gory photo of a photojournalist who'd lost an eye to a rubber bullet. A medic tent, cops viciously stabbing their water bottles, bandages crumpled at their booted feet. Her latest repost was a resource guide for staying safe while protesting:

1. *Wear a mask and keep it on. You will be in close proximity to others and also potentially yelling/singing (which may increase risk through increased projection of viral droplets).*
2. *Carry hand sanitizer. If you can't get to a place where you can wash your hands, this is very important.*
3. *Plan for possible exposure to chemical irritants . . .*

Plan for possible exposure to chemical irritants. There were a dozen more items on the list, but Amudhini didn't want to read them. Reading Shruthi's posts were often guilt-inducing on multiple fronts . . .

They'd had a dream of a summer, but when fall came, the cooler air brought tensions with it. September was a time for making plans, setting goals, and it turned out they didn't want the same things. Hard enough to merge two people's dreams—adding a third and fourth made it exponentially more difficult. In the end, Darnell had gone off to med school in Connecticut, and though they tried to keep things going for a few months, long distance was never easy. Shruthi had followed him in the end; Amudhini and Stephen moved out west for grad school.

But Amu often wondered if the four of them might have survived if Amudhini had tried harder. They'd heard it often enough back then that it had become a mantra: communication is rule number one in a poly relationship. That applied to a monogamous marriage too of course. You had to open your mouth and talk about what was bothering you, hurting you. Shine a little sunlight on the wound, give it a chance to heal. But it was so much easier to stay silent.

Shruthi was always a deer, dipping a graceful head to drink from the clear spring at the rocky edge of the pond. And Darnell, a monarch butterfly. Not the creature Amudhini would have picked for him but somehow perfect—beautiful and fragile and rare. They'd spent weekends cooking ridiculously elaborate food, feeding it to each other. Then falling asleep a sweaty tangle in the bed, eight arms and eight legs finding space to coexist, to live a second life in shared forest dreams.

Shruthi had just started training to become a psychiatrist then; sometimes she would start talking about Jungian archetypes, a collective unconsciousness. But all they really knew was that together, they were magic, living outside the rules of space and time and society.

Twenty-five years later, Amudhini still ached at the loss. She closed Shruthi's posts and shifted attention to the garden club group, a refuge.

Amudhini still had a dozen tomatoes to get in the ground and not enough sunlit space for them. She tried to remember to water all her seedlings daily, but the day slipped by faster than seemed possible, and sometimes she forgot only to be confronted with a withered leaf or seed mix gone dry and hard. She hated the waste of all that initial time and care, a living thing starved of what it needed to survive.

After somewhat frenetically starting thousands of seeds two months ago, Amudhini had mostly managed to accomplish the deaths of many seedlings. You could skip watering them for a few days if you'd spent the extra money for a self-watering tray, but eventually, seedlings needed care. One proverb claimed, *The best fertilizer is the footsteps of the gardener*—you had to actually walk through your garden regularly or, in this case, walk down to the basement with its grow lights, so you'd notice which plants had started to droop.

She'd tried to get the children to take over that duty, but they seemed to need prodding for everything these days. Roshan grumbled at every additional task added to his chore board, heaving heavy sighs that made Amudhini want to scream. Meena mostly hid up in her room in the attic. Amudhini fretted that her teenage daughter might be slipping into depression up there, all alone for hours, but Meena insisted that she was fine. She was mostly keeping up with her schoolwork, and if she actually spent most of her time FaceTiming with her friends and watching TV, Amudhini didn't have the heart to yank her away from that comfort.

Someone had posted a method for string-growing tomatoes, which was more compact than using cages, but you needed tomato twine, which she didn't have. These days, every purchase came with the question of whether it was better to order online (more cardboard to smother the planet, more time saved) or go to a store (more health risk to them all, more support for a local business). Exhausting calculations, and often, she chose the easiest path, pushing down the guilt. She'd wait to make a decision about the tomatoes, giving them a little more water to get them through the day. Maybe tomorrow things would be clearer.

Stephen and Amudhini converged in the kitchen, assembling lunches of leftovers. Amudhini said, "We need milk. I can walk to the store . . ." Her heart already lifted at the thought, a few blocks' walk down the street, perhaps waving hello to neighbors from six feet away.

He frowned. "Can we manage 'til tomorrow? I can put it on a delivery order for the morning."

Amudhini took a quick breath, biting back annoyance, and said, "Yes, we can manage." There was some powdered milk buried on a shelf still. It wasn't good, but it would do.

If it were up to Stephen, they'd huddle together in this house for months on end. When Amudhini had brought up the possibility of renting a few weeks at a lake house for the summer, he'd immediately said those beaches were too crowded—didn't she remember the last time they'd gone? And he'd been reading about the disease more, the long-term consequences for even asymptomatic children—

Amudhini had cut him off, not needing to hear any more. *Fine, that's fine. Never mind.*

You were supposed to compromise in a marriage. If her husband lived at 1 on the caution scale and she lived at 3, then they'd have to try to meet somewhere. And closer to his side than to hers. 1.5. 1.2. That was only fair since he was the one who thought the risk was greater, but sometimes it was hard to bear.

Amudhini could've asked Stephen to help with the weeding, but they'd survived the last three months by giving each other as much space in the house as possible, so she was working alone with a podcast to distract her. She should've gotten up earlier, done an hour before the heat of the day descended. Now Amudhini suffered for her sloth, sweat trickling down her back, breath coming hot and miserable under the mask. Sometimes she didn't wear the mask when working in her own garden, but that carried its own penalty; inevitably, Amudhini was stabbed with guilt whenever someone stepped into the street to get a little farther away.

She pulled up nutsedge and quackgrass, chickweed and lambsquarters, listening to an interview with chef Alice Waters. Waters said that we'd been lied to, that beauty wasn't about spending money. She said, "Beauty is the language of care."

Wasn't that why Amudhini's father had cut mangoes for them, peeling the fruit carefully, why she did the same now for her family? Every day for the last few weeks, now that mangoes were in season, Amudhini had peeled mangoes for her children, leaving a full plate on the counter. She'd remind Roshan to leave half for his sister and would keep only the seed for herself, the parents' lot. A small note of joy and grace, a gift to the little ones in a hard time, when they'd lost so much, more than they realized.

Waters would surely know which of these weeds were edible. When so many were enduring economic hardship, it felt particularly terrible to waste food. The dandelions Amudhini had pulled a month ago had made a tasty ice cream. Flowers rinsed, petals removed and steeped in boiling water, petals strained out, and the dandelion water blended with honey. It tasted like herbs and sunshine, like summer around the corner. Dandelion root was supposed to make a good ice cream too, reminiscent of coffee.

They'd often cooked together, the four of them. That was one of their particular joys, the pleasure of quibbling over just how much cayenne to add to the curry, endless attempts to bake the perfect sourdough loaf. The boys took up brewing that summer, hauling vats of boiling water up and down the apartment's back deck stairs to the shared backyard, and while Amudhini couldn't make herself like beer, Darnell and Stephen had brewed her a beautiful honey mead.

One night, they all ended up on the back porch late, huddled under sleeping bags, well past tipsy and not caring that they were being eaten alive by mosquitoes. Shushing each other—"You'll wake the neighbors"—but Shruthi was a screamer. Amudhini covered Shruthi's mouth with her own, swallowing down Shruthi's pleasure while the boys took care of business, trying not to laugh out loud with the sheer joy of it all.

They'd fallen asleep out there eventually, exhausted from their efforts, and met again in dream. That night, the two girls explored the forest, Amudhini riding on Shruthi's haunch, discovering a waterfall, a starlit meadow, a cave—and then fleeing an angry bear. They'd woken up laughing and, consumed by itching, rushed inside to slather calamine lotion on each other's backs, which inevitably led them back to bed.

Two podcasts done; time to switch tasks. Amudhini dumped the weeds in a trug and hauled them to the backyard compost bin. She didn't have time or energy to turn them into something delicious today. Amudhini had back-to-back Zoom meetings for the next six hours, and the family would have to fend for themselves. Some days, all they ate were peanut butter sandwiches and cereal.

To get to the compost bin, she had to pass the big burdock she'd asked Stephen to dig out. It still stood, getting taller every day, that nasty taproot getting longer and threatening to send up its gorgeous spiky flower. It was tempting to leave it—would be easier. But the problem was that it'd soon set seed; you'd end up with a garden full of burdock and not much else, prickly thistles tearing at your clothes, shredding skin. Some plants needed digging out if you wanted a garden instead of wilderness.

Some ideas were equally pernicious, embedded in the fabric of their lives. That's what Shruthi was doing, posting and posting and posting, somehow finding the time in between her telemedicine calls with patients, trying to counter the messages, change people's minds. Sometimes Amudhini tried too, but there were days where the effort felt overwhelming. How did you fight state-sanctioned violence, embedded in hundreds of years of bitter history, emboldened by the tacit support of so many who benefited from the disparities? Was a social media post really going to make a difference, or was she just avoiding any real effort in the battle? Their enemies were entrenched, overwhelming.

Stupid burdock. Amudhini stared at it, trying to assess if she was strong enough to dig it out. She did most of the gardening, and her arms had some muscle under their layer of fat, but Stephen was still stronger. Stupid biology. He'd probably forgotten about digging out the burdock—yesterday he'd been swamped in union meetings, trying to find the language to convince administration to hold onto jobs for the non-tenured faculty. Important work, and it certainly helped that he was a tenured white-male math professor pushing fifty. They needed him in that room. But it still grated that Amudhini would have to remind him about the digging. In a long marriage, you learned to let such things go, but it was harder now, trapped in close quarters for so long.

The Japanese considered burdock root a delicacy. Maybe Amudhini would ask Stephen to try to save this root when he dug it out—she could probably make a little time to cook it tomorrow. It would be satisfying to eat an enemy.

Another group text: *Reminder: Bridge at 5; wear masks.*

Just a few hours away.

Darnell had posted to his Facebook story: *Yesterday was like walking into fire. Today, there are flames on the side of my face.* The story posts were like the kids' Snapchat—going live and disappearing in twenty-four hours. Darnell rarely posted anything permanent, too wary of possible blowback at work. *Walking into fire.* He might be talking about the disease or about the protests or more probably both. Amudhini ached for him, wishing there was more she could do to help. She couldn't sew masks for more than two hours a day; her back started to ache. Her body had limits.

Waters was right about the importance of care. But the problem was that so often care took both energy and time. It took time to stand at the counter, peeling mangoes for the children. It took time to make a nice dinner out of garden weeds instead of leaving the kids to assemble their own sandwiches.

You could sometimes buy extra time with money—they'd hired a biweekly cleaner for their home, and that might have been the best thing they ever did for their marriage. But they'd been paying the cleaner for three months now not to come, not wanting to put her and her children at risk. Roshan had learned to clean the toilets, true, but half the time, Amudhini ended up asking Stephen to redo them because at ten Roshan just wasn't very careful.

What did you do when money couldn't buy you time, when the world was on fire and everything needed care? Eventually, you ran out of both time and money and were forced to triage. Yet there was no ethical way to triage human lives: a disabled person's life was not worth less than the able-bodied. The elderly had so much more weight to them than a child, so much knowledge and experience that might be lost too soon. Yet who could bear to let a child be at risk?

It hurt her heart, knowing that Darnell fought his way through that morass every day, writing up plans for how his intensive care unit would handle triage, praying that his staff wouldn't be faced with those choices. It never should have come to this—one full riot suit for a militarized police officer cost as much as fifty-five suits of PPE for healthcare workers. Darnell even had to decide who needed the scant PPE more, the nurses or the doctors or the front office staff. Impossible decisions, yet someone had to make them. It had fallen to their butterfly, fragile and beautiful and rare, trying to weigh the value of human lives in a world that seemed to count his own Black life as worthless. And then he came home exhausted to Shruthi and their boys.

A few years ago, Darnell and Shruthi had moved to the same town as Amudhini and Stephen, settling just six blocks away from Amudhini's house. Yet the gap between them felt impassable.

Before dinner, Amudhini and Stephen chivved the children into a walk. She was grateful they were old enough not to complain at the need for masks, despite the heat. They were all getting plumper, losing conditioning trapped within the confines of house and garden. Though it was churlish to complain, given how much space they had compared to the neighbors in the apartment building next door.

The children skipped ahead, arguing amiably about some project in Minecraft, and Amudhini reached out, took Stephen's hand in hers. He curled his fingers around hers, squeezing lightly. The tensions of the day had built up, but thankfully they dissipated in this, the touch of skin to skin.

After the foursome shattered, dissolved into two pairs after they'd all hopscotched around the country for grad school and jobs, there had been a bad year. She and Stephen had broken up. Amudhini had lived all alone for months, alternately weeping and writing; at times, she'd felt like she was going mad from skin hunger. How many were suffering that now, trapped alone in apartments, dutifully following the rules? Sometimes Amudhini saw a friend walking across the street, and the urge to run over and hug them broke over her like an immense and brutal wave.

She and Stephen had found each other again, and somehow, a small miracle, managed to get jobs in the same city, the same university. And then Darnell got his job at Rush, and he and Shruthi had moved back from the East Coast, settling in this small suburban town. Two decades gone by, and they'd all finally wanted the same things: good schools, restaurants, and theater. A queer-friendly town, which wasn't directly relevant to their lives these days but still mattered to them all. And what if the children didn't end up straight? Too early to tell, but wise parents planned for the future.

Ethnically diverse too. It certainly wasn't perfect on the racial front, but this town had a strong history of fighting against discrimination, enacting legislation to resist white flight, welcoming immigrants. The children's public schools were full of biracial and multiracial kids. There weren't so many places where you could raise mixed-race children in relative safety in America; it wasn't such a surprise that the four of them had all ended up here.

They'd invited Shruthi and Darnell over for dinner when they first arrived in town, the children sent to share pizza and video games in the basement. Darnell insisted on bringing fried chicken, the recipe he and Amudhini had developed together—the one she'd never managed to make properly on her own. The first bite of spicy, crispy skin brought tears to her eyes. It was too late now to go back; they'd chosen different paths, settled into safe, conventional domesticity. Had they really wanted such different things back then? Or was it just hard being four instead of two? Life was easier when you stopped fighting the current.

The younger kids rattled back up the stairs, interrupting their coffee and reminiscing. Roshan ran over to tug at her sleeve. "Mom, can we walk to the park? Mali plays Pokémon too. There's a gym I've been trying to take down, and I bet I can do it with him to help."

Mali was a few years older than Roshan, tall for his age, though still skinny. Amudhini said, "You're done eating already? Well, it's okay with me if it's okay with his parents."

Shruthi frowned at the pair of boys. "Mali, only if your big brother goes too. You don't pay enough attention when you're caught up in that game." She glanced outside and added, "It'll be dark soon. I want you boys back in thirty minutes."

Darnell added, "Hey, Mali. See if Roshan has a jacket you can borrow, something brighter." Roshan was in his customary bright red, but Mali wore a black Star Wars sweatshirt, hood hanging down. In that moment, her vision blurred, and Amudhini saw what Darnell and Shruthi must always see—how dark their younger son's skin was. Her Roshan was so much lighter with Stephen's genes in the mix. Stephen saw it too—across the table, his eyes widened.

"Sure!" Roshan said. "He can wear my yellow Pikachu jacket."

"Perfect," Darnell said, smiling. A little tension going out of him, invisible to the boys, but even all these years later, Amudhini could see it. If she could, she would have reached out to take Darnell's hand, pull him close, hold him tight until their breathing matched and he was calm, at peace. But that wasn't her place anymore.

"Tell your sister to go along too," Amudhini added. It was all she could think to do. Meena would sigh and barely repress a complaint, out of respect for the visitors, but with her along, the boys should be even safer. If Amudhini had married another Sri Lankan, the way her parents had wanted, would she make these calculations every night? Every day, every night, she took their light skin for granted.

There had been a few meals together after that one, promises to get together more often, soon. It was hard though, so busy with work and the children, all of them. Legitimately hard, which conveniently let them avoid too much awkwardness. The past was long ago and difficult to discuss, and after all, they'd settled into their marriages over the last few decades. Easier to bury it all.

They were solidly together now, she and Stephen, even if shelter-in-place had added a light layer of tension. Solidly middle-aged too. Her friend Angeli had written online: *We are middle-aged now. These protests are often violent, and if you can't run fast, don't go. You'll be a burden on those already there. But it's also true that since we are middle-aged now, some of us have resources. We have money. We have access to the system. We have the ability to follow up this season of protest with political organizing.*

All true, and no one would chastise Amudhini for staying home today. Shruthi would never call her up and demand that she go.

Yet here they were. She'd taken them walking toward Shruthi's house, turning right and left under the leafy trees. Six blocks, and as they'd come closer, Amudhini could feel herself slowing as if she were wading through tar. She could still turn back; no one would know. And even saying the words to Stephen was hard—silence was easier. *Silence equals death.*

They'd protested together almost thirty years ago when there'd been a gay-bashing incident just off campus. Cut pink triangles out of cloth, asked students and faculty passing by to pin them to their clothes, hosted a sit-in outside the administration offices, pressuring them to extend domestic partner benefits to LGBT students and staff. Shoulder to shoulder, hand in hand. They'd won that fight. Stephen had been with her then, unhesitating, but now, everything was different, everything was harder. They had so much more to lose.

The kids, a few steps ahead, stopped outside Shruthi's house. "Hey, Daddy," Roshan called back. "Isn't this where Malik lives? Do you think we could go for a Pokémon walk?"

"Not a good idea," Stephen said. "We need to give it a few more weeks at least, make sure we're well past peak. Sorry, kiddo."

"That's okay," Roshan said, shrugging. "Hey, Meena—race you to the corner!" And they were off, young and vital and full of life, impossibly beautiful. How could she risk them?

If things had gone differently though—it would be *her* children with ebony skin, carrying all the weight of what that meant in America.

"I want to go to the protest tonight," Amudhini said, pushing the words up out of her dry throat, bracing for Stephen's resistance. She'd argue him into it—and if she couldn't persuade him, well, she'd go anyway. She had to, no matter how upset he became. Amudhini thought they were solid enough to survive that.

But Stephen surprised her. "That's important too. Just . . . be careful."

She nodded, squeezed his hand, released it. He called to the children, "C'mon kids. Time to head home." Amudhini turned away from them, walked up the path to Shruthi's door, pressed the doorbell with her elbow.

Shruthi opened the door, surprise evident in the arch of eyebrows. "Amudhini?"

Amudhini said, "Are you walking to the bridge? Can I walk with you?"

"Of course." A smile on her face and a spark between them—connection re-established. "Here. You can carry this sign." Shruthi held it out: *No justice, no peace.* Any peace in this country was an illusion built on others' pain.

Amudhini stepped forward, holding her breath—close enough to hug and, oh, not hugging hurt—took the sign in hand, stepped back. Six feet. It seemed impossible that they could maintain distance while protesting, but she would try her best. Maybe being outside would protect them enough.

Shruthi locked the door, and they started walking in the street, the only way to walk together and maintain distance. Others came out and joined them, more and more as they approached the bridge, a flood of black T-shirts, hand-sewn masks, homemade signs. One young girl held a sign up high, a sign plastered with the dark faces of the murdered, and Amudhini's heart broke all over again. Then they were at the bridge, hundreds at least, pressed close, pressed together, shoulder-to-shoulder. She should be worrying about the pandemic, but she had no space left for that in her heart.

Amudhini turned to Shruthi, and the world shimmered around her, the heat of the day blurring the borders. Yet this was no dream. Their magic had entered the waking world. And Shruthi was no gentle fawn—no, she'd grown to a stag over the last two decades, mighty and many-antlered, fire in her eyes. Ready to defend or, if needed, attack. Her voice roared over the crowd, fiercely leading them in call and response:

Whose streets? Our streets! Whose streets? Our streets!
No justice, no peace! No justice, no peace!

If we don't get it . . . shut it down!
If we don't get it . . . shut it down!
Show me what democracy looks like!
This *is what democracy looks like!*

Amudhini uncoiled herself, scaled form slithering, and threw back her dragon head, roaring with the motley crowd of furious creatures. There was magic here—and power too, even if she didn't understand it. For her children, for Shruthi's children, for the dark-skinned children Amudhini might have had if she'd made different choices all those years ago, she had to take the risk.

If they stood together, they could change *everything*.

§

Mary Anne Mohanraj is author of *A Feast of Serendib* (Mascot Books), *Bodies in Motion* (HarperCollins), *The Stars Change* (Circlet Press), and twelve other titles. *Bodies in Motion* was a finalist for the Asian American Book Awards, a *USA Today* Notable Book, and has been translated into six languages. *The Stars Change* was a finalist for the Lambda, Rainbow, and Bisexual Book Awards. She's a recipient of an Illinois Arts Council Fellowship in Prose, has received a Locus Award and a Breaking Barriers Award from the Chicago Foundation for Women, and has been Guest of Honor at numerous conventions.

Mohanraj's other publications include stories for George R.R. Martin's *Wild Cards* anthology series, the SF/F anthology *Survivor* (Lethe Press), *Invisible 3* (co-edited with Jim C. Hines), *Perennial: A Garden Romance* (Tincture), stories at *Clarkesworld*, *Asimov's*, and *Lightspeed*, and an essay in Roxane Gay's *Unruly Bodies*. She is currently working with Rad Magpie to develop a video game based on 5th-century Sri Lanka: *Sigiriya*.

Mohanraj founded the Hugo-nominated and World Fantasy Award-winning speculative literature magazine, *Strange Horizons*, and served for ten issues as editor-in-chief of *Jaggery*, a South Asian literary journal (jaggerylit.com), which she continues to publish. Mohanraj has taught at the Clarion SF/F workshop and is Clinical Associate Professor of fiction and literature at the University of Illinois at Chicago.

Mohanraj lives in a creaky old Victorian in Oak Park, just outside Chicago, with her partner, Kevin, two children, and assorted animals: www.maryannemohanraj.com.

SACRED SHE-DEVIL

Craig Laurance Gidney

R uby Spurlock was the third sister murdered in as many months. According to the article, Ruby had been found in a remote area of Rock Creek Park with her neck slit, and there was evidence of sexual violence. The article, like so many papers, opted to use Ruby's deadname, a final violation of her memory. One officer made a point of mentioning, "People like Mr. Spurlock were known to engage in illicit sex work," and that such work had inherent risks.

Opal sighs, disgusted and weary at the same time. But she doesn't indulge in the emotion for too long. There is much important work to do.

She lights a homemade candle, shaped like a pyramid and infused with the essence of lavender and rosehips. The flame dances, an orange teardrop in the darkness. Behind the candle is the altar of Pomba Gira, the sacred prostitute. On a wooden shelf, there is a chalice filled with cachaça upon which float rose petals. Two aspects of the Pomba Gira sit on either side of the silver cup. A doll with smooth brown skin and a frizzy cloud of hair stands on the right side, clad in an opened crimson cloak that reveals her unashamed nudity. A necklace of skulls encircles her neck. On the left side is a doll with skin the same color as the other one's cloak. She is also nude, and two horns jut from her forehead. The flickering candle flame animates both figures.

Opal says, "Ruby Spurlock, please come to me. This is a safe place. A sanctuary for gender warriors!"

Silence, like a dip in pressure, mantles the room. The flame flutters and distorts the shape of the dolls, stretching and squashing the attendant shadows. Opal feels tingles in her spine, a rill of needles.

Someone is listening.

Opal begins to sing Ruby's name over and over, turning the syllables into a joyous tune, a celebration of Ruby's life.

The flames dance to the rhythm of the invocation.

The shadows of the two aspects of Pomba Gira merge into one shadow, a shape both voluptuous and demonic—a horned silhouette of a goddess. The bodies of both dolls become dewed with moisture and appear no longer porcelain or plastic but skin-like. Skin in tones of obsidian and ruby. The room fills with the scent of incense, redolent of nutmeg and allspice. Already warm, the humidity in Opal's room grows until her forehead is beaded with sweat. Darkness thickens in one corner—into the shape of a woman.

"Oh, Ruby," says Opal, "my sister, don't be shy. Show me how fabulous you are!"

Color blooms in the darkness, slowly resolving itself into tones. The finished woman doesn't completely materialize. She's transparent and beautiful, a tracery on the gloom.

Ruby Spurlock has red-brown skin and long box braids that fall to her waist. She's in white culottes and a mint-green peasant blouse.

Ruby takes a tentative step forward. "What is this place?"

"This is my apartment. And as I said, a sanctuary."

"How did I get here? And why do I feel so weird? It feels like I'm on Special K. You didn't drug me, did you?"

Opal stands up, moves toward the apparition. "How much do you remember?"

"What do you mean?" Ruby says.

Sometimes this happened. A soul would block out the trauma of their passing. For most, it was a blessing. Sequestered in the afterlife, they moved through memories, traveling through time and space with mood the only compass. How and why they crossed over was not relevant, so it was often forgotten. Opal had no desire to reintroduce the violence of Ruby's death, but it had to be done. Other lives were at stake.

"Forgive me, Ruby. For waking you up. But I'm gonna need you to remember your last moments."

"My last moments?" Ruby says, her tone halfway between amused and terrified. "I can't feel my legs or arms. You *must* have drugged me!"

"No, darling. I'm afraid to tell you that you have passed away . . ."

The shade of Ruby flutters like a moth against a lit candle. Her form wobbles and blurs.

"Stay with me, Ruby. I need to hear your story."

Memory seems to come back to her. Her face crumbles, overwritten with terror. Widened eyes see something that Opal cannot. Ruby's face blooms with bruises, and her skin splits, leaking blood. Her eyes blink in rapid succession as her murder plays out once more on her phantom flesh. Opal wants to look away, but she cannot. Ruby is a sister, and it's Opal's duty to guide her through this experience, to bear witness. So she watches the violation, a weird pantomime, sees each shiver of terror and gasp of despair as death rains down on Ruby's body. Her skin records each imprecation, becoming a testament to abuse. The monster who did these depraved acts is invisible, seen only by Ruby. It seems to go on forever until the light in Ruby's eyes fades out.

Then Ruby is no longer in that terrible moment. She has not survived but now exists in another form.

"The motherfucker raped and killed me," she says, her voice wavering much like her spectral form.

"I'm so sorry you had to relive that, sister," Opal says. "I wish I could hold you and comfort you— "

"Oh, yeah?" Ruby says. She's now more shadow than image, hidden in the corner of the room. "If I could, I would kick your ass. I was at peace when you pulled me here to your shitty little hovel. I was in Paris, walking down a runway beneath the Eiffel Tower, wearing couture clothes. People were clapping for me and handing me bouquets. I was a fucking supermodel! Then you had to drag me back here to remind me that I was killed by some maniac."

"I'm sorry, sister, but —"

"I am *not* your sister. You are way too common to hang out with the likes of me. Send me back!"

Opal stands, suddenly feeling shabby in her floral house dress. Her hair is unbrushed and hidden beneath a red headwrap. She has a faint mustache that won't go away, even with all of the hormones she's taken. She is far from being fashionable.

"I will send you back," she says, careful not to let any irritation creep into her voice. "But first, you must tell me what your killer looks like."

Ruby huffs, "I don't know, bitch. He looked like a million other mediocre white dudes. Why do you want to know?"

"So that we can stop him."

Ruby is silent for once. She asks, "Who is 'we'?"

Opal sighs. "That's a long story. Bear with me. I used to be a sex worker . . ."

"You mean you were a whore," Ruby says with venom in her voice. "No more of this PC 'woke' shit. You sucked dick for money."

Opal ignores Ruby's rudeness, though it's hard to do so. "I was a whore," she continues, "and I was good at it. Very good. And because of my, let's call it unique anatomy, I was very much in demand."

"You mean, you're a chick with a dick."

Opal cringes but, at first, refuses to rise to the bait. But anger gets the best of her. "I couldn't afford the surgery. It's not like I had a Cadillac insurance plan."

"I know that's right," Ruby says. Opal can't figure out if she's speaking in cynical solidarity or being sarcastic. She decides that it doesn't make a difference.

"One of my clients—johns—was a repeat customer. Let's call him Sam. Sam worked in international finance, and one time, he offered to take me with him to São Paulo. I'd never been out of the country, and I didn't know when I'd have the opportunity again, so I paid for an expedited passport and went with him.

"We were supposed to be there for the better part of a week with an excursion to see Iguazú Falls at the end. I had the time of my life, eating, drinking, and shopping like a princess. He had long meetings in the daytime, and I spent the time drinking caipirinhas like a fish and exploring the city. We stayed in a fabulous hotel—with a balcony room that overlooked the city. São Paulo goes on and on as far as the eye can see. Tall buildings, bright lights everywhere you looked. It's like Manhattan multiplied! Little shantytowns, called favelas, are in the shadows of high-rises."

"It sounds extra," Ruby mutters.

Opal laughs. "It is extra. The population is something like 20 million, at least twice New York City's. It's also twice as busy. And twice as dangerous.

"Well, one night, Sam and I got into a fight. You see, he wanted to 'share' me with one of his colleagues. And the colleague was into some things that I don't do . . ."

"Bondage and domination?" Ruby asked.

"No, girl," Opal says. "I can handle whipping and yelling at white dudes. It was stuff like golden showers and strangling. Stuff I'm not comfortable doing. And I told Sam that in no uncertain terms. Well, he offered to pay me more. I still refused. I'm not into piss play!"

"He wasn't respecting your limits," Ruby says.

"He called me an ungrateful bitch. Then said I could find my own accommodations."

"He kicked you out?" Ruby's shade flickered. "What a douchebag."

"A total fuckboy move. I left the fancy hotel with $100 dollars in Brazilian reais, my luggage, and my passport in a country where I didn't know the language. I was angry and also scared to death. São Paulo isn't the safest place, mind you. I was a sex worker, but I had my pride. But somehow, by the grace of God, I found a place. It was a hostel on the border of one of the favelas."

"So a sketchy place."

"Yes. But you know what? It wasn't bad for the first two nights. I was the only person there, so I had the place to myself. I was in the women's section in a room of bunk beds, and I had the shower all to myself. The desk clerk, João, was a real sweetheart. He couldn't have been more than twenty-two. He had lovely olive-brown skin and the greenest eyes I have ever seen. He practiced his English with me and told me a little about his life. He was from a small beach town in the north of the country, a place called Praia de Iguape, and moved to São Paulo because there were no jobs there. I could tell that he missed it. He told me that he had a sister who was "a girl like me." I was unsure of what he meant at the time.

"It all changed on the third night when a group of German tourists took over the hostel. They were two men and two women. I was taking my afternoon shower after being out and about when one of the women passed by the shower stall and saw what she saw. Of course, Heidi—or whatever her name was— freaked the fuck out, and she told her friends about me.

"That evening one of the men, let's call him Gunther, who could speak English well enough, told me I couldn't stay in the women's room and made a big stink of it to João. João, bless his heart, was completely unfazed. He calmed those assholes down and then told me I could stay, at the same rate, in the empty apartment above the hostel. He told me that I was a child of Pomba Gira, whatever that meant, and I was lucky to have her favor. I thought it was an odd thing to say, and mind you, his English wasn't the best, and my Portuguese was non-existent at the time.

"The upstairs apartment was amazing—and not just because I had my own bathroom. It was tiny, enough room for a twin bed. The walls of the room were painted a beautiful ruby-red pomegranate color. The floor was tiled and wonderfully cool, given that the place wasn't air-conditioned. In a corner that might have been a tiny closet, there was an altar.

"There was a table covered with a cloth the same pomegranate color as the walls. In the center, there was the foot-high figurine of a red she-devil, naked as the day she was born, her tits out and proud, and with a mischievous sneer on her face. She had horns, yes, but she was in no way demonic. In fact, she was *cute*. The figurine was surrounded by melted wax candles along with an unopened pack of cigarettes and a half-empty bottle of cachaça. At the time, I didn't understand the significance and thought that the display was like the Brazilian equivalent of the Tiki gods. You know, some Pier One imports kind of shit.

"My last night in Brazil, I decided to go out. I mean, fuck Sam. Why the hell should I not have a good time? João told me about a good sushi place and gave me directions. I managed to order the food without embarrassing myself and even treated myself to some sake.

"Well, not *some* sake. I had two lychee-flavored saketinis along with a couple of shots."

"Go ahead, girl," Ruby says. Her form is more substantial now, looking less like a hologram.

"I got *turnt* and got lost on the way back to the hostel. One street looked like another, and before too long, I found myself stumbling into one of the favelas. There were no streetlights overhead, and the pavement was uneven. The buildings looked haphazardly put together, made out of corrugated tin, shipping containers, and cracking concrete. The only lights came from candles, kerosene lamps, or strung up Christmas lights. Feral cats slunk about, and the narrow streets were empty.

"I wandered around, going down streets, hoping to find some place I recognized. But it was no use. I turned around one corner and saw a group of four or five young men, around João's age. They were all huddled up, puffing weed cigarettes, whispering and laughing. One of them saw me. I moved away from them, but they could see that I was lost and afraid, so they surrounded me in a vaguely threatening manner.

"Of course, I couldn't understand them, but I could guess that what they were saying was lewd because their voices were rowdy. They egged each other on, flashing grills and gold teeth. One of them draped his arms across my shoulder in a painful grip.

"He began stroking my hair. The others closed in on me. And I knew that it was only a matter of moments before it got so much worse. I felt that mixture of helplessness and rage I'm sure you're familiar with."

Ruby nodded her assent.

"I braced myself for the worst, a fight I would almost definitely lose.

"Then we all heard it. The clop-clop-clop of high heels on uneven pavement. The gang fell silent. So did I for some reason, even though it would be the perfect moment to yell for help. I think that I was surprised at the loudness of the sound. It was definitely a brazen gait.

"The footsteps stopped, and around the corner, there came a woman. Though the word *woman* does not really do her justice. She wore stiletto heels that made her tower over everyone, which she would have done even if she hadn't worn them. The heels themselves were sharp and transparent, like icicles or glass shards. She could have easily slit a throat with them if she needed to. She wore a gown the color of pomegranates, an off-the-shoulder gown that glowed like a neon sign. Her hair was a storm cloud of black curls, rippling in an unfelt breeze. Her skin was soft brown, her lips luscious and dewy. She had large breasts that defied gravity. And her eyes—they were black. Blackety black. And ancient, like a piece of onyx yet to be mined.

"The woman took in the scene before her. Then she threw back her head and *laughed*. Heartily, a throaty staccato chuckle. 'You boys are looking for trouble. But trouble has found *you!*'

"She spoke in Portuguese, but I could understand her—every word. The gang member who held me said something that was probably not nice, definitely crude.

"'You couldn't handle us with your tiny, little worm-like cocks. I can smell your nasty crotch from here! What did you all do—wash them with shit?' she asked.

"Another gang member called her a long chain of something that probably included the C-word. And she, in her pomegranate glory, said, 'My vagina is sacred. Your diseased bird dicks would shrivel up inside. I am the eater of little boys who think they are big men!'

"The man who had grasped me let me go and lunged for the strange and apparently insane woman in the red dress. He grabbed her forearm but immediately jumped back as if he had been stung. His hand was red and smoking. She laughed that machine-gun laugh of hers—head thrown back, laughing wildly.

"Another gang member spat at her. She fixed him with her cobra glare, and I saw the ring around her pupils turn red. The same color as the room where I now stayed. And I knew then that she was the real version of the she-devil doll in the small alcove in my room. Her divinity rolled off her in invisible waves.

"'Leave both of us alone,' she shouted. 'Leave at once! Or your dicks will be flaccid slugs for the rest of your miserable lives. Your balls will shrivel to the size of raisins, and your cum will stink of rotten fish!'

"The gang was inching away from her at this time. One of them flashed a switchblade.

"'Your little metal dick is worthless,' she said. And the blade flopped over as if it had melted. She began to dance, some variation on the samba that incorporated lots of twirls. She spun faster and faster, like a whirling dervish. The pomegranate fabric of her dress unspooled and got longer and longer until it became snakes, red cobras that struck out at the retreating gang."

"That's some crazy story," Ruby says, now glowing in sharp definition. "I wish I'd had a guardian she-devil."

Opal wished that she could have touched Ruby, held her hand, comforted her. She said, "She has many names, but the followers of Quimbanda and Umbanda call her Pomba Gira. She's the patron saint of girls like us. She can't bring you back to life. But she can avenge you. And save other sisters."

"So she's the goddess of ratchet hoes?"

Opal laughed. "In a manner of speaking. But she is so much more! We are her children."

Ruby's form shimmered, winking in and out of the liminal shadows. "I have one question," she said after a while. "Can she fuck him up?"

§§
Craig Laurance Gidney is the author of the collections *Sea, Swallow Me & Other Stories* and *Skin Deep Magic*, the novella *The Nectar of Nightmares*, and the novels *Bereft* and *A Spectral Hue*. His work has won the Moonbeam and IPPY Awards and been nominated for the Lambda Literary Award.

PURITY

Nadia Bulkin

Purity was more beautiful than he expected her to be. She rose like a graceful concrete minaret above city center, one skateboard-sized foot flat on her podium while the other dragged behind in perpetual mid-push. Her right hand pressed to the stone folds of her stone dress where her heart should be, if she had one, while her left arm tumbled forward as if out of a reverie. She looked a bit like an opera singer. But not a shrinking chorus girl. The motherfucking lead.

Her full name, according to the poster he'd snuck out of his father's study before he left for college, was *Purity Holding the Heart of the People*. In the poster, she was striding across the countryside, leading an army of tiny citizens—town mice, country mice—toward an unseen but brilliant future. And so too did Kip hurry across the street to get closer to Purity, dodging motorbikes and minivans painted with the names of neighborhoods that he vaguely—oh so vaguely, like the vestiges of a dream—recognized from his childhood. But Purity he couldn't mistake. He knew her in his soul. From the moment his father first sat him on his knee and explained that the pretty lady on the poster was neither real nor fictional but a dream of what could be if only men were good—she had been twice-stitched into his heart.

After spending the morning at his father's gravesite, Kip needed something good to focus on. He was dazed. Heat-struck. The cemetery had been so oppressive, weighed down by the wet heat and the lamentations of distant mourning parties and by Uncle Amin who in his silence made it very clear that he did not forgive Kip for missing the funeral. Kip thought about reminding Uncle Amin that he *had* been back for his mother's funeral five years earlier but quickly reconsidered.

"There was a revolution," Kip tried to explain as if his uncle was the one who'd been watching it on international news. "No one was flying in. We were under an advisory." And Uncle Amin just stared back at him as if to say, *You should have found a way.*

Three hours into the torture session, a centipede started crawling over his father's grave marker, and Kip started to sway, so Uncle Amin nodded and let him go. So Kip hurried. Away from the moody banyans, the wailing women, that centipede, the tiny horrible grave marker that he could barely read. No, his father wouldn't have wanted an ostentatious mausoleum with a crying angel— his pride was too quiet for that—but that tiny slab felt too small to carry the memory of a man who'd loomed so large in his life. Slumping in the taxi, the unhappy truth dawned on Kip that even columns fall and turn to dust, and that was when he truly regretted not finding a way home.

Only when he was back in the city did the squeeze on his body loosen. He could breathe. Buy a cheap soda. Listen to a dumpster drum troupe. Consider buying a "Revolution!" T-shirt as a gag gift for Jeannie but change his mind in embarrassment. Pop the kink in his neck, settle into his skin. It felt better looking forward. The country had been waiting so very long to look forward.

Kip had been wandering toward the voice of a man yelling into a microphone, some activist with a fruit crate—calling for "A nation that is built on justice for all"—when he saw her. Purity.

Why everyone else loitering around city center wasn't gawking at her, he could only guess. The kids on mobile phones probably hadn't spent years nurturing a sanctified image of her, maybe weren't so shocked to find that thought-cloud birthed into stone. Kip, though, drank her in. He circled her, reached out to touch her and then demurred. He read her bronze plaque, still new enough to sparkle in the sun: PURITY HOLDING THE HEART OF THE

PEOPLE. Just like his father's poster. That poster had been *illegal* back in the day. Anti-government ideas and all that.

A little tingle—or was that sweat?—rolled down Kip's spine. So they got her built after all, the unattainable dream. They must have moved at back-breaking speed; Julius Marlin had only been forced from office the month before, and already, here stood Purity, reminding the people whose heart she was holding of what they were all striving for. No more kickbacks, no more graft, no more public funds paying for the First Lady's diamonds. Incorruption. Clarity. Light.

He wished his father could have seen her.

Here in the revolution's backwash, Kip had his pick of hotels. Even the swanky five-star places had cratered their prices along with the economy . . . well, the ones that were still open that is. Most of the name brands—the Shangri-La, the Hilton—were "temporarily closed." A few had been burned and stood like charred carcasses against the skyline. It wasn't like anyone was coming to visit the city anyway—no one except the occasional lost boy, trying to pick up his father's inheritance before it was surrendered to the hunger of the newborn government.

Kip had chosen the Pacifica, mostly because it wasn't foreign-owned, and it felt in some small way like a contribution to the local economy. The receptionist had seemed so very glad to see him, offering him his key in her clammy hand with an exaggerated bow. Maybe that was why they put him all the way up on the eighteenth floor with a pitiful gift basket.

"Have a wonderful stay," she said, eyes to her desk, "sir."

It saddened Kip a bit. He was one of them, wasn't he? He might have an American apartment, but his passport was still hunter green. Then again, the Pacifica was built to be window dressing for a very particular type of play that was reserved for men of a very particular status. In the old days, this was the sort of place he might have peered at from the backseat of his father's car, wondering how high the ladder of the world went. Into the sky? To outer space?

Looking out his eighteenth-floor window, Kip still had no idea how high humans could climb. All he could tell was how very far he could fall, how many bones he might break. *Stop. Breathe.* He shut his eyes, pressed his fingers to his temple—*inhale, exhale*—and to steady himself, fixed his gaze on a giant flag hanging from the corpse of a half-built skyscraper—*inhale, exhale.* He was trying to call back that high-flying hope he'd felt in city center, that rush of vigor and purpose and life that he got when he laid eyes on Purity. *Breathe in—*

He squinted. Was that Purity peeking over the buildings? God, he hadn't realized she was so tall. She hadn't *looked* that tall. Maybe he was just closer to city center than he thought? It was amazing how crowded the city had gotten since he'd moved away—how crowded yet so small, streets opening inside streets, city blocks dividing like cells of a rapidly growing creature.

One of his college roommates, Travis, used to say that his Purity poster reminded him of *Attack of the 50 Foot Woman*—one of many cultural references Kip didn't know he was missing, having grown up with state television. Except Purity wasn't crushing cars on a highway. Purity wasn't attacking anything except, well, forces of *im*-purity, the corruption and lies and theft that defined the Julius Marlin regime. And even then, she never attacked with violence: she just stood, unarmed and beautiful, daring them to give up their moral authority by striking her first.

He did not explain all this to Travis of course. And by the end of the year, he thought it was funny, almost adorable, to think of Purity as this B-movie icon, a supposedly timeless and universal symbol who was actually locked in her own time, shielded with the innocence that came with always being new. Purity would never compromise. Purity would never spoil.

Kip only realized that he was still holding his breath when his laptop started to chirp. It was 12 p.m. in Guavatown, and Jeannie was on her lunch break. She looked sweaty, bug-bitten, pallid now that she'd moved up from digging wells to supervising the digging of wells.

"I'm . . . orry"—her face splitting and then knitting together again—"nection is ter-ble."

"It's okay. Thanks for calling."

"I heard it's—" and then Jeannie warped. Her jaw dislodged, and her eyes blurred as if they'd been partially erased. Kip clicked around on the screen, trying helplessly to unfreeze her. In a moment, she was human again, breathing, blinking, scrutinizing something on her computer. She didn't seem to have realized what had happened to her. "Is there a curfew? Is it safe?"

The way she said *safe*—like it was a color-coded classification, God how development people loved quantifying things like *safe* and *free*—made him want very much for this not to turn into another one of Jeannie's failed states. "It's fine," he said. "No curfew. No problem. Everything normal. They're even putting up their own statues."

Jeannie stared at him in what looked like disbelief, her eyebrows raised and her mouth ajar. But maybe that was just the internet glitching out again.

After Jeannie went back to work, Kip went back to the window. He wasn't sure why, but he needed to check that she was still there. Purity. And she was, lit up by the waxing moon.

He clicked his tongue, chiding himself for forgetting his camera that afternoon; his old phone had jammed up every time he tried to take a picture in city center, leaving him stuck with the last dutiful photo he'd taken of his father's barely readable grave marker. He should try to swing by city center again before his return flight. Get a shot of Purity in eternal bloom. He'd regret not having one. At least, he was pretty sure he would.

Purity. From this distance, he couldn't see her face. He pulled the curtain closed.

In truth, Kip was not cut out for revolution. He used to cry during riots as a kid; even as a grown man, when he first heard about the scale of the September Protest that had turned into the September Revolution, he threw up. He suspected that was why his father had sent him abroad after high school and probably why his mother had gone along with it. He could imagine the conversation: *It's too dangerous for him here. He'll never make it. We have to protect him.*

Thom, his father's lawyer, was no revolutionary either. Kip distinctly remembered his father ranting in the study and Thom refusing to engage except to try to quiet him—as if it was the government pressed up against the door instead of Kip who was just hoping to go see Purity.

Thom was something else entirely: he was a survivor, literally. His home village had flooded, and he'd been orphaned at the age of twelve. The sort of world-upending catastrophe that either breaks a person, anoints them, or turns them into a jack-of-all-trades who can adapt to any crisis, any change. And there was real value to Thom's ability to shapeshift, especially since "law" under the Marlin regime had been less a bedrock than a wriggling snake. He might have sworn to uphold a whole book of contradictory nonsense, but survival was Thom's only real law.

Thom was the one who warned Kip that the state was going to start liquefying accounts held by non-residents, and he had to come and physically collect his inheritance now. Kip wondered if his father had griped to Thom about his idiot son, pursuing a dead-end career in the arts. Either way, it was kind of Thom to warn him. It meant Thom wanted him to survive.

They met their contact in the Ministry of Home Affairs parking garage. The old days of treating a government desk like a cash register were gone; the clerks who used to look the other way were watching now. Their contact was pretending to be on a smoke break.

Kip didn't know where Thom found the guy; he looked terribly unhappy to be handing over a letter authorizing a withdrawal of funds. Even after Thom paid him his "advance," he kept giving Kip sour looks. "What are you going to do with daddy's money?" he asked as if he was calculating the number of schools that wouldn't be built now that the state couldn't spend Kip's inheritance. "Buy another car? Get a new house? Cruise around the world?"

"I don't know," Kip said. "What are you going to do with your cut?"

The official snorted and turned back toward the Exit sign. "Just go home, boy."

Thom and Kip went to his father's bank, produced the letter, and made the withdrawal. As the sleep-deprived bank teller counted out hundreds of thousands of depreciating dollars, Kip wondered what Purity would think. Imagined her peering in through the windows with her enormous blank eyes, frowning in disgust at this final gasp of elite corruption.

Afterward, Thom took him to a nearby noodle stall for lunch. "We're celebrating," Thom said, pulling a flask out of nowhere, but Kip didn't feel like it. He shifted on the crooked stool, trying to discreetly adjust the envelope of cash, acutely aware of the way the cook was staring at him and the fact that the only other person under the tarp was one mall cop slurping at a bowl.

"You all right, Kip?"

"Yeah." He cleared his throat. The cook looked away and lit a cigarette. "Thom, you know that statue of Purity? Do you know who put it up?"

Thom squinted, tilted his head as if shaking out pool water, and said, "I'm sorry? Purity?"

"Yeah, the statue. *Purity Holding the Heart of the People.*" Kip pantomimed

Purity's iconic hand gestures. "She was this . . . pop symbol of a possible revolution before you could really talk about a revolution. My dad had this poster in his study . . ."

"Oh, God. That was all your father's shit," Thom said, waving his fork. "Not mine."

"I'm just surprised they got it built so fast."

For several ticks of his knock-off Rolex, Thom just squinted at him. "Nobody's building statues," he finally said, sounding like he was talking to Child Kip. "They're drafting laws. They have to write a whole new constitution. I'm sorry, co-write—have to make sure all the little mountain tribes are okay with it." He scoffed. "You can imagine what a mess that is."

"Okay, so who built the statue in city center?"

Thom started chuckling. Even before he replied, Kip could feel the answer on a molecular level. A deep truth wriggling along the bottom of his stomach, the same gnaw he felt when he got the call that his father had suddenly dropped dead—a reminder that no matter where he went, he'd still be in this haunted funhouse of a country, still smashing into mirrors, still running from a monster that was still right behind him, waiting for him to take the briefest rest.

"There is no statue in city center. It's just plantains and pigeon shit. Sorry to disappoint."

But that wasn't disappointment weighing down his guts. It was something much more primal than that, much less complicated. Something heavier. Something a lot like stone.

It was true, what they said about transportation breaking down without the iron stopwatch of the state. But it was also true that there was a greater ease to people's bodies, a slackness to their smiles—even if those grins were just a bit too toothy and the teeth just a bit too sharp. It was like someone had taken a hammer to the state's power and sent the pieces flying off in all directions for anyone to grab. The shards might be just as sharp, but at least, they were smaller.

Thom had left him stranded at the noodle stall with the shifty cook, saying he was late for a meeting with a new client—some "poor unfortunate," Thom said eagerly, "screaming about something." Before he hurried off, he breezily told Kip to stay away from the "murder cabs."

"Which ones are the murder cabs?" Kip asked because when he was a kid there weren't any—just the baby-blue taxis owned by the one company that had bought off the government.

"No medallion!" Thom yelled over his shoulder. Except *none* of the cabs had any medallions, which meant *all* the cabs were murder cabs. It was like all the baby blue taxis had vanished along with the government, and now there was only a sea of red-and-yellow murder cabs calling out to him in low, drawling voices: *"Hey . . . mister . . . where to?"*

So Kip and his heavy inheritance tried to take the bus, and when the bus never showed—or maybe he just missed it, some of these old city buses limped along dangerously close to the curb with no names, no numbers, no destinations—he started to walk.

It was supposed to be an hour walk down a few main roads named after long-dead generals, but his phone kept redirecting him, taking him down nameless alleys and backed-up service roads, once forcing him to hop across a gurgling ditch—as if it was following some other map, a buried one hidden beneath whatever dressings and bandages the interim government was frantically wrapping around the bleeding country.

Here in the unglorious dark, too far from city center to hear even the rumble of victory speeches on microphones, pictures of the disgraced President Marlin hung like phantoms. Some were defaced with horns or blacked out like any other cursed image, but others were faded, taped to the insides of darkened windows as if once upon a time they'd protected the people within.

He felt a tickle at the back of his neck—like a whisper, a dare—and quickly glanced over his shoulder, hoping to see nothing in the alley. Please no muggers, please no gangsters, please no soldiers. And thank God—not even a stray cat. But then he made the mistake of looking up, and there, peeking between rooftop antennas, was Purity.

For a good minute, Kip tried to rationalize her presence. Her new and terrible size. His brain twisted the city up like a wet rag, collapsing what he knew were miles of streets into just a few city-blocks, telling himself, *It's okay,* when it was very clearly not. He turned, took a few steps, checked again—and she was closer now, her face lit up as if on fire by the flickering red-neon sign of a cheap hotel. She was looking at him. Wasn't she? Staring at him without eyes.

Jeannie once asked him why political ideals were always personified as women. Liberty, enlightening the world. Columbia, dragging pioneers westward.

Britannia, ruling with trident and shield. He'd been sketching wartime pin-up girls for the Eversweet contract and said something glib about obsession with the female form. But Jeannie suggested something else as she looked over his shoulder at Eversweet Girl #3: "Or maybe it's because they can't move."

Purity was moving. She was past the hotel now. The red light was a halo for her shadowed face. Only God knew how—it wasn't like he was seeing this enormous statue drag its feet against the asphalt, and it wasn't like he was hearing screams, but oh, she was moving, somehow she was—but Kip knew why. He could see her now for her malice, the cruelty of her face, her indifference as she destroyed. She is a knife, he thought. She is a guillotine blade.

And I, Kip realized, *am rotten meat. A sickness. An impurity. A scoundrel who ran from his homeland and let his parents wither there alone. A coward who watched as his fellow people gave up their bodies to build a dam big enough to slow the wheel of the state. A scourge.*

Kip did the same thing he'd done since he was a child: he ran. Like he ran from the sound of flash bombs and the sight of army trucks and the whole damned motherland when he was seventeen. He lost sight of everything: direction, time, traffic, the envelope of cash. Only one truth in his head, the only ideal he was upholding: *Don't look. Don't look at Purity.*

Kip woke and immediately slapped his hand against his heart, feeling for his pulse. He had lost it in his sleep; he had become stone. He'd dreamt of being anchored on Purity's pedestal, reaching toward an empty horizon with a frozen hand. KIPLING HOLDING THE HEART OF THE PEOPLE. Below him, a sea of people pushed and pulled at each other's bodies, none of them paying him any mind. Only one face stared at him, and that was Purity. Hair knotted, lips chapped, eyes red. Where had she been, this Purity? He imagined her climbing over fences, running with scuffed knees through the unquiet night. He imagined her breaking rules. Fucking up. Childishly relishing the misfortune of another. He imagined her changing.

He found his pulse, and it immediately started to slow. As he lay in bed with the Pacifica sheets pulled tight over his head, Kip finally started to remember some things. Like the fact he was probably dehydrated and had only had a bowl of noodles the day before. And the fact he'd taken a full course of anti-malarials before getting on the plane, despite Jeannie's urban legend about a grad student who stabbed his host family while under the influence of quinine.

He couldn't wait to leave. He imagined the relief he'd feel when the plane kissed the tarmac, when he stepped into the cold recycled air of the airport terminal and knew for certain that he would never have to step foot in this haunted country again. And because there is no rest for the wicked, as soon as his body started to unclench, he saw his poor dead parents patting him goodbye at the airport. Nodding, knowing their boy would never be a hero.

Traitor, he thought to himself. *Coward*.

Miserably, he threw the sheets off—and that was when he saw her. A pale gray human-sized shape at the end of his bed. A bilious scream crept up hot and bitter at the back of his throat, and he threw up on the floor. All the time he was vomiting, even with sweat dripping in his eyes, he kept her in his line of sight, but Purity didn't budge. So polite. After a few dry heaves, he sat down on the bed, facing her. Exhausted. Defeated. Unable to pick up and run.

Purity looked different now. Not only because she fit in the hotel room when the last time he saw her she would have been able to crush him in her fist. No, also because she looked melted. Featureless. Like an old statue that had been scraped and picked at and left to the mercy of the elements for hundreds of years. She too looked defeated. Less like a warrior-princess and more like a ghost with a sheet over its head. And not just any ghost. His ghost. The sister he never had. The child he left behind to grow up in that old, gated house in the old, decrepit regime.

And this thing she held clasped to her chest as if to absorb it into her calcified body was—whose heart? His? He put his hand to his heart again, just to check, and as he did so, two words filled the room: "I want." It wasn't a voice. It was smoke, seeping in under the doors. "I want."

Kip didn't wait. He reached over to his nightstand and grabbed his sketchpad, his pencil. He started to draw Purity as he first saw her in city center, striding bravely against the forces of corruption, her right arm pressed to her heart, her left arm reaching, pointing, letting go.

No. It wasn't right. She wasn't right. Too graceful, too rigid, too beautiful, too inhuman. That was Purity as he remembered, not Purity as she wanted.

"Again," came Purity. So he tore the page off as if peeling away a top layer of skin, digging deeper, digging in. On the blank page—bare as a bone and just as dry—he started anew.

§

Nadia Bulkin writes stories, thirteen of which appear in her debut collection, *She Said Destroy* (Word Horde, 2017). Her short stories have been included in editions of *The Year's Best Weird Fiction*, *The Year's Best Horror*, and *The Year's Best Dark Fantasy & Horror*. She has been nominated for the Shirley Jackson Award five times. She grew up in Jakarta, Indonesia, with her Javanese father and American mother, before relocating to Lincoln, Nebraska. She has a B.A. in Political Science, an M.A. in International Affairs, and lives in Washington, D.C.

A TECHNICAL TERM, LIKE PRIVILEGE

Bogi Takács

I get home and the rental needs to drink my blood. Again, always, the fourth time this week and it's only Wednesday. I strip off my top, undershirt. I'm not going to take off my pants, I don't care what the rental thinks. Does it think?

I think it only feels, feels a deep resentment of humans living inside its caverns, its air bubbles. Housebeasts have sensory nerve endings on the inside, feel us tickling them as we live our petty lives, squeeze us for blood.

The life of flesh is in the blood, the preachers say. The housebeast doesn't need my blood, type O, good for transfusions. It needs the magic. But most people, their magic is sparse, less heavily invested in their body. The housebeast needs the blood, to squeeze out every drip of sustenance—not from the blood itself but from what it carries.

While tentacles slither around on my skin, while the wall glues itself to me, I wonder for the fifth time what I can do to get out of this. I feel my bone marrow straining to produce more red blood cells. I need a break. The wall grabs a lock of hair, and I know it's a total loss—I'll have to cut that one off too. Should've just worn a cap, should've cut it all short—should, should. I need to call the rental office.

Twelve apartments in this beast, or was it fourteen? The third beast on the block, a student neighborhood. It was all right before the semester started. I don't know what the new students are doing, but the beast needs so much more magic now. Are people puking in the disposal-holes? Trying to squeeze out broadband from the beast-nerves?

The worst part of it is, it feels good while the beast drinks. It needs me, yes, but I can feel that it loves me. It wants to keep me close.

I stagger away from the wall, rubbing my bruised skin, crashing onto the sofa, staining the cover. Too tired to take a shower, but at least we'll have enough water pressure now. My hand is searching for the receiver, and it helpfully pops out, shakes drips—of what, synovial fluid?—off of itself. I groan into the receiver, ask for the rental office.

"Yes, I understand it needs the magic. Yes, I understand these were the terms when I signed. I was"—I take a heavy breath—"just wondering if it needs to be so . . . direct. I mean, I can give it magic without the blood. I can do that."

I scratch the side of the receiver with a stubby fingernail. It squirms. I'm too faint to understand the explanation from the chirpy person on the other end of the line in an office somewhere nearer the head. But it's a no—it's always a no. "The contracts aren't written with someone like you in mind, you have to understand," but heck, they need me if they want to keep the beast going. Maybe they should recruit from the Department of Applied Magic and not from, I don't know, engineering students.

Then again, I didn't go into magic either. That shit is for the highborn.

I fall asleep, wake a few hours later. I am late with my homework in Entirely Useless Studies, but I can't muster the enthusiasm. A graduate degree, yes. Your fellowship will pay your tuition, yes. But all the money I get from teaching on the side goes into renting this room that I couldn't even call a cavern. And the food, the iron supplements lately, those cheap industrial hotdogs pushed out by a factorybeast. I hear some of the highborn mages are vegetarian, and I wonder how they swing it. I need to get another twelve-pack of eggs, low-cost protein. I wonder if I could raise chickens without the rental office noticing. Is chicken feed cheaper than eggs? Chickens smell though. I wonder how long I'd last before I roasted them on a spit—live for today, don't mind tomorrow.

By the heavens, I'm hungry. I rub my face, but that doesn't summon food. I find my last hotdog in the cooling pouch. I eat it cold, can't wait out the minute to warm it up. I need to shower. I need to go. I saw this flyer on campus, and maybe it can be just the thing.

I run my fingers along the words. I feel scrubbed. The hot water was great in the shower—never mind it took my blood and sweat to boil it.

ONWARD TO ARMS! FOR THE REVOLUTION!

The Communards of Szederkei County invite YOU to our Campus Meetings . . .

The address is off campus but close by. Some university official probably ousted them. No one wants to deal with a bunch of rabble-rousers, well, except the rabble-rousers like me. I crunch the leaflet back into the pocket of my robe.

Two tall, pale dudes are by the door, and I feel acutely scrawny. Possibly also insufficiently cis. But that's not what they complain about. At least, I *think* it's not that, though one never knows really.

One of them fingers my pendant, and I flinch from the touch. I had too much touch today already, even if not the human kind.

They say something about no mages—and I can't quite make it out, I'm worse off than I'd thought—and I get into a debate with them. One of them just keeps on repeating that mages are a privileged class. As if that was some technical term, and for all I know, it is.

"You can do something other people can't. That's a privilege."

I can't even muster a glare. I feel like I can't do anything because I've been sucked dry of every last drop of blood. And I can't argue well either because what, I mean, he's technically right. I can do things other people can't.

I walk away wordless, but a debate rages in my head. All the highborn mages, that's privilege. But why can't I. I mean I can. Maybe it's just that I'm a failure. I wanted to pick myself up by my bootstraps, get a fellowship, study Useless Studies—I mean mathematics. (I actually love it. When I can keep my eyes straight to stare at a page.) Get into fights with engineering students, grow up, get into grad school, stop getting into fights. Moan about engineering students and how they vomit into every available receptacle after a night of drinking and more fights. All while I need to make sure the housebeast has enough energy to digest all that crap. I'm sure I did the same as a first-year, but that was before the rental hikes, before grad students got pushed out of on-campus housing.

I was better at fights, to be honest. Still not late for a career as a cage fighter maybe, but I value my brain cells, and I can't afford the protective enchantments.

Rika stares at me over their bagged lunch: a sandwich of what, bread and cheese probably. They're looking tired today, colorful hair hidden in a hastily wrapped scarf, their skin patchy pink. "Stop thinking about witty repartee," they say.

I shake my head. I've been thinking of so many rejoinders. I could've yelled at those people that I was trans, but if they didn't guess, wasn't that also *privilege*? What if they did guess? It wasn't like I could quiz them. "How did you know?" I ask Rika.

"It's all over your face," they chuckle, their voice dry. "Staircase wit, it's called. You come up with it when you're already walking down the stairs."

"Well yeah, other buildings have staircases. Mine has an esophagus."

"You could unionize." They just toss that out there as if that was so easy.

"What, a renters' union?" I'm laughing.

"Exactly that." They're frustrated with me, I can feel. Their mind vibrates. They put down the sandwich and lean forward. "I'm not studying sociology because it's so good. I'm studying it because I want to beat them at their game."

A blanket *them* that can cover everyone. From greedy landlords to Revolutionary Communards.

I shake my head. "I couldn't even get into a proper resistance meeting."

"Eat something. You'll feel better." They tilt their head. "Want one of my sandwiches?"

"What's inside?"

"Um, bread and cheese?"

I take it.

At home again, my turn to squeeze broadband out of the nerves. I read and read, and all I conclude is that everyone has their own jargon, subversives included. I feel resentment toward *the apparatus of revolution*. I'm not the right kind of comrade, and I feel I can't even complain.

Even if I could find a new place mid-semester, which I couldn't knowing my luck, who's to say it won't go exactly the same? I used to live on Butchers Row in the inorganic housing before it got demolished, and at one point, the floor cracked open, and I found myself knee-deep in my downstairs neighbor's ceiling just like that. Another housebeast, and that'll probably go the same. Every place that has an opening this time of the year will probably be salivating for magic. *The beast or the owners,* I wonder.

Am I the only one in this situation? I don't know, but I guess everyone else who might be is probably likewise flattened out from all the blood loss.

I glare at the dark-purple walls, the rugged, ribbed interior of the housebeast. Why does it need me? I can't even hate it. I feel bad for it. It's trapped same as I am. It needs my cheap blood filled with magic and whatever power comes out of a hotdog after it's digested. I'm surprised my terrible diet hasn't poisoned it already.

Well, that would certainly be a way to take revenge on the rental office. Or just to make the argument again that I could be doing this without the blood. Maybe that would convince them.

I half cough, half guffaw. Instead of pamphlets, I could be reading about the biochemistry of housebeasts.

It takes effort to find out which substances can accumulate in my blood with less harmful effect to me than to the housebeast. Everything takes effort when I'm so woozy, lying on the sofa, scratching my still-churning belly. Exhaustion can look a lot like laziness, and I only hope an idle rental clerk isn't looking in on me via the beast's internal photosensor cells. It can be done.

I hope I'm not interesting enough.

It takes even more effort to find a substance I can easily add to my diet. I've never stolen food, and maybe it's not the best to begin when I'm keeling over from anemia and a distinct lack of magic. I budget and rebudget. The numbers don't add up. Maybe Rika has a thunderfruit tree in their back yard. Maybe I can find a restaurant that gets rid of a few pounds of a very specific mushroom every day. Maybe, maybe. I could use my magic for this if I had any left over after feeding the beast. As if.

I feel like dirt for even contemplating harming a living creature, but I can't keep up this feeding schedule. It's not about hurting an animal for fun. It's about bare survival. Would I slaughter a cow to eat it? Oh yes, I would. I'm an inveterate city dweller, but I'd give it an honest try if the need was pressing. Is this so different?

I scribble numbers on my slate. I look at an Intro to Pharmacokinetics text. I make guesses about my metabolism. Fuck if I know how magic affects all this.

Two full measures of thunderfruit a day while minimizing other liquid intake. That shouldn't be so hard. In just a few days, this will cause striking cutanous symptoms on both interior and exterior membranes. Of the housebeast, not of me. Worst case, I might get a mild rash. Diarrhea from all the thunderfruit.

If I time it well, skin will slough from the ceiling straight into people's breakfasts. I wonder if I can adjust it so that it happens in the offices near the head first, where the rental company is safely cocooned.

Public databases are a close second to magic. Here are all the public trees on city plots. All the fruit-bearing trees. All the thunderfruit trees. Here, watch me draw a path connecting them all. If I take one from each, I'll have two full measures per day easy, and no one will notice. You're not supposed to harvest them, but you can take for personal use.

My personal use is just a little more demanding is all.

Here is the path. Only three Imperial miles on foot. Per day. While my bone marrow cries in agony as it grinds away at producing new blood cells.

All my limbs hurt. By the second day, I know I'll have to involve somebody.

I explain my plan to Rika, sitting in the park at a chessboard, pretending to play. I connect imaginary dots.

"Once they realize my blood is useless for the beast, they'll surely allow me to give my magic without giving blood. I just have trouble getting enough thunderfruit."

They shake their head. "What's to say they won't just boot you from the rental?"

A sudden pounding ache in my stomach. I can feel my magic going askew. I must *believe* in my plan, but Rika . . . Rika is so sensible. They're probably right.

"Believe me," I say, but I can't believe myself anymore.

I'll just have to stop talking to Rika. Stop talking to anyone. *I will be my own internal revolution,* I think to myself as I mash the thunderfruit together in a bowl, shovel it into my mouth. It is gooey sweet and just vaguely medicinal, that kind of pharmacy aftertaste.

Two measures of thunderfruit a day is an awful lot. Bodybuilders do this with rice and what, chicken? I'll think of this as my spiritual discipline. I should believe in the kindly powers, but the kindly powers had never so much glanced at me; they stranded me with enough magic to be sucked dry but not enough standing to become a mage. Not the right family, not the right gender, not the right anything. What is the right gender even.

The housebeast skips a day with its requests, and another. Is it suspecting something?

My blood stews. Then my guts churn. I didn't think about this—will my excrement poison the beast even faster? I considered everything so carefully. How did I miss this? I should've gone into Useful Studies, like medicine.

I drag myself to the academy and lock myself into one of the restrooms there, near the Department of Complex Systems where no one ever goes anyway. I think wistfully of my research projects, now abandoned. I am my own project.

There is a sticker in the toilet stall, telling me where to look for help with domestic violence. There is no sticker about being eaten alive by your rental. I still wonder about reaching out. Does this count? Surely there has to be a limit to how much blood can be extracted from a person on a regular basis. My contract only specified something vague based on "needs and capabilities." It's just my luck that I'm probably the most magical person in this particular housebeast. It's like not having enough bandwidth because there is only one outgoing nerve bundle for the whole floor.

I stumble against the door when I try to exit the stall. I'm not one for religion, but even I think about invoking the kindly powers.

Rika has left a message while I was gone, and I ignore it. I can't risk being discouraged.

As I topple on the sofa, I feel a pang that's something new, not my upset stomach or my head foggy from blood loss. I feel a need, and I'm not sure if it's the beast's or mine. It feels good, being fed on, after all. And for three days, I've gone without.

I laugh bitterly. The housebeast beckons.

This is the time. Breakfasts and convoluted schedules are irrelevant. Now is the time.

May the kindly powers help me. Help us all.

I peel off my shirt, tearing a strap in the process. I fumble with my undershirt, sprain a finger that I hooked under it just wrong. I laugh-cry. I lean against the wall, and the wall leans against me, tentacles reaching out. Even my own smell feels different. Has the change in my metabolism been so drastic already?

The housebeast drinks deeply and pauses for a moment—

It retches the blood out in a spasming stream onto my floor and my half-full, half-empty backpack.

I sit on the floor, a familiar numb shock, and time passes and passes and passes until someone from the rental office comes by to draw my blood, test it. I offer my arm without words.

"You have a week to make sure your numbers are within range and your blood passes the filter," the clerk says chirpily, her hair arcing straight around her face as she tosses her head to the side. "Otherwise, your contract will be terminated at the end of the week."

My mouth moves finally, slowly. "How am I supposed to find a place mid-semester?"

Filters. I didn't think the beast would have filters. What do they filter out?

The clerk says something that's not even apologetic.

"Can I give. My magic. Without the blood. I can do it. Just look at my results," I croak and beg.

I don't understand the answer beyond the *no*.

"Can I please. I promise I can do it." I raise my voice.

"You need to stop threatening me," the clerk says.

I'm small and half-covered in my own blood and feeling like I'm about to die. *I'm not* threatening *you*, I think—but I don't say anything. She's read me as male,

I know. As someone potentially threatening. I don't want to give the company yet another reason to boot me from the rental.

She is going on about how they're going to make sure it'll all go on my record. Something about the police. Something about one last chance to get my act together and stop drinking that filth that passes for alcohol in the alleys near the academy. One week. Or she'll make sure—*you have to understand it's not about your person*—that my "violent behavior" gets reported.

That wouldn't put an end to finding a room. It'd put an end to my studies, to everything I've scraped together all this miserable life.

I want to pace the room, but I can't. Mopping up the blood has used up all the energy I had left. I lie on the floor, convinced there's still a puddle underneath me, but I can't.

Why do they need my blood?

"The kindly powers have saved you from me," I tell the housebeast and chuckle. "They've saved you, not me." My abdominal muscles spasm from my attempt to laugh. Speaking is hard. I can just think at the beast—we are connected well enough at this point.

I don't want to hurt you, I think. *But I can't keep this up.*

The beast is so hungry.

You're in a bad situation too, huh? I turn to my side, fetal position. Even my thoughts are hard to sustain. *In a reasonable world, the rental company would just hire some mages to deal with the shortfall.*

What is it that my blood does that my magic can't?

Rika finds me on the floor, and I'm muttering the same question to them.

They always take me seriously. They answer, talking to me while they're sponging me down, feeding me with something refreshingly solid. Rice cakes?

"Giving your blood ensures you don't have enough energy left to rebel," they say. "You have more than enough magic to cause a mess."

That's certainly possible. I nod.

"And also . . ." They fall silent, bite their lower lip. "Divide and conquer. If you can be kept away from other people fighting for equality, so much the better for the people in power."

I blink at them.

"Don't tell me you bought into this bullshit take on class struggle." They glare at me. "I'll be blunt with you. Magic doesn't make you into an aristocrat."

"I still pass as male," I say weakly.

"Look, take this from one trans person to another, all right? You don't pass anywhere near consistently, I'm sorry. And do you even want to? I mean, you're not a man exactly."

I groan. "My gender is a mess."

They wave at me. "Your gender is just fine. You just need some stability in your life. Look, you're trying to convince me how privileged you are just as you are in the process of being slowly eaten alive. Can you have some compassion for yourself?"

I will not cry. Am I crying? "I tried to hurt the housebeast."

"That's the same thing. You think of the housebeast as your opponent, not as your comrade."

"It is trying to eat me . . . ?"

"It's hungry because it's been deprived of resources. That's my best sociological analysis really."

I stand up, immediately dizzy, and sit back down. Rika is right. Terribly, terribly right. "Why are you helping me?" That's not what I want to say.

"You helped me out back in first year, and now I'm helping you out." They pause. "But to be honest, I'm just telling you this so that you can feel satisfied. I know that for you it's all give and take. But sometimes I just want to help out my friends. I can't stand to see you all alone, working yourself into a small desperate corner."

I try to protest, but Rika is still right. They don't have much magic, but their thoughts move along such orderly lines that they pull my own thoughts along.

After Rika leaves, I lay down to sleep, but it's as if some kind of barrier had tumbled down inside me, and instead of dreams, I join—join the housebeast.

The housebeast is hungry and sad and disappointed and frustrated and hungry and disappointed. Heck, now *I'm* hungry.

The housebeast has an immediate response to run away, to fly—

Hold on, I think at the housebeast, at myself, *running away would solve precisely nothing. Where would we go? What about your other inhabitants?*

I am treated to a plan of all the inhabitants' movements, a time-lapse, points of minimal and maximal activity—

You've thought about this, have you?

Was *I* keeping the housebeast from running away? I was a prime source of sustenance. But I could send magic remotely if with some additional difficulty . . .

That's why it had to be blood. If people were allowed to feed housebeasts with pure magic without a carrying substrate, anyone could go anywhere. Housebeasts could go anywhere. Broke grad students could go anywhere. Societal control would be loosened.

I'm starting to think like Rika.

I can feed you without the blood, I think at the housebeast, *if that works for you.* My magic replenishes faster than my red blood cells at least. *We won't have to tell anyone. We'll just pretend.*

The housebeast doesn't quite understand *pretend* and is hungry, so hungry.

We can sort it out. I shrug, my shoulders shot through with pain at the motion, my awareness abruptly recentered on my body. I have just eaten— my last hotdogs if memory serves. I can do this. I tell the housebeast, *You can feed.*

Do I sleep, or do I just blink off, I don't even.

I know when I wake that something is askew. I drag myself to my feet, and the floor tilts. I fall. My left ankle cracks. The startle blanks out the pain. I don't have a window—windows are only on higher levels—where's the door? I'm in some random shirt and underwear and naked legs, and it shows how bad the situation has gotten. I can't be bothered about the legs. I half walk, half topple out the door, and it opens with the usual smacking sound, but there are some weird harmonics in it that I can't quite tease out.

I crash into the rental clerk with the fancy hair. We all have our ways of trying to hold on to something that makes us feel human, I suppose. I understand her all too well for a moment, and I wonder if I have too much magic left, if that can even be a thing.

"The anchors have detached," she says. "All shards have failed." And this has to be a technical term too, like *privilege.*

I feel ridiculous. What did Rika say, something about revolution being structural change that cannot be achieved by any one individual's heroic actions, something something? This is bad. Is the housebeast flying? The housebeast's flying after taking enough power from me to tear off the anchors and rise to the skies. So now we'll probably get shot down with anti-air cannons for all I know. My one-person rebellion—how privileged. How pointless.

"I've let it loose," I mutter. "Sorry, I didn't mean to." But truly, did I?

The clerk stares at me, and no, I can't make out her thoughts. The floor wobbles and I feel a pull, a pull at my guts, or at least something somewhere inside me—

"You fainted," the rental clerk says. Am I on the floor? I must be. She's somewhere out of arm's reach. It makes sense. She doesn't dare to be closer to me.

"No one's thinking about anything," I tell her, and in my head, this makes sense too. The beast didn't think this through—a characteristic of beasts of all sorts. I didn't think this through.

Even without the blood, the beast will fly and drain me and drain and . . .

"Almost everyone is out at this hour," she says. "So I figured it had to be you. Of course."

"Structural change," I say with brutal effort, fighting my mouth gone rubbery numb. "We need to descend. Do you know how to steer?"

"Steer what? They are supposed to be anchored—"

Rika would surely have an amazing idea. There is no plan, nothing, just my need to get away from it all that the housebeast has clearly internalized. A big, giant cursing that fills the skies. The kind of pointless anger that makes the rental clerk flinch away from me as I stagger to my feet. I still don't know her name, but I can't move and speak at the same time, and something's got to go.

The beast didn't digest the poison, but something made it through the filters after all. Something that's grimy and base as only emotion can get.

I'll hate myself in the afterlife, surrounded by the kindly powers gently but insistently telling me off.

I only know this, am only driven by this—I need to at least see for myself what's happening before we all pancake on the ground.

The front gate is so far. It opens, opens, and I'm stunned. I expect the rushing air, but there's some kind of giant flap that had extruded out of the wall, and it's keeping the worst of the impact off me.

Also, we are close to the ground. Uncomfortably close. Tears the snot out of my nose close.

Are we right above Rika's housebeast?

I brace for impact. The clerk at my right loudly prays.

Down just below, I see the other housebeast's front gate open, and I cuss.

Rika looks up at me, our eyes lock across the distance like they shouldn't, and Rika's incredulity makes it across whatever connection we have built, mind to mind.

Their beast wobbles. Moorings detaching? Rika ducks back inside. Are they whooping? They must be. I'm not sure how I can tell through the noise, must be the magic. Their beast is eager to join mine. Something draws them together. Pheromones or possibility? Magic, physics, wait maybe that newfound social context—so hilarious as to feel plausible. Wrenching really. The beast breaks loose from the ground with a crack I feel in my teeth.

"This structural enough for you?" I scream at the top of my lungs, and I laugh, laugh as my housebeast swings low and up again on a neat parabola as Rika's housebeast gains speed and altitude as all around us the masses of cheap rentals detach from the ground, take to the air.

Every jug of water has that one last drop before it overflows, I find myself thinking. The conditions were here: the hungry beasts, the grip of control loosening its hold. I'm just one person, and the heroic deeds are for another, but out of the mess, this emerged, and maybe others can make sense of it.

The ocean's near, so near, and all I can hope for is that when I pass out, we'll be above water and maybe, just maybe, free once and for all.

§§

Bogi Takács (e/em/eir/emself or they pronouns) is a Hungarian Jewish agender trans person and an immigrant to the US. E is a winner of the Lambda Award for editing *Transcendent 2: The Year's Best Transgender Speculative Fiction*, the Hugo Award for Best Fan Writer, and a finalist for other awards. Eir debut poetry collection *Algorithmic Shapeshifting* and eir debut short story collection *The Trans Space Octopus Congregation* were both released in 2019. You can find Bogi talking about books at www.BogiReadsTheWorld.com and on various social media like Twitter, Patreon, and Instagram as @bogiperson.

A Field, a Shadow, Indeed a Shadow

Margaret Killjoy

The thing about being the weird girls is everyone just kind of lets you get away with weird shit. Up to a point. Usually that point hovers somewhere around felony. Which meant that I was about to get us into trouble.

Someone had torn down our fort. Okay, they'd torn down the forest around it too, and I suppose in a cosmic sense that was the bigger deal, but I hadn't spent half my eighteen years laboriously building the fucking forest.

They'd clear-cut the whole thing. Or at least several acres of it. I have no idea how big an acre is really. I can't picture it. They'd fucked up a lot of forest. Like a whole neighborhood's worth of forest. All gone. Nothing left but dust and dirt and branches. And the ruins of our fort.

It hadn't even been personal. They'd done it with bulldozers. No one had scaled the—admittedly precarious—flagpole and torn down our rainbow flag. No one had gone through the effort to graffiti some hate-crime shit calling us queers. Hell, no one had even bothered to rob us. Nic had spent hours and hours and broken not a small number of laws assembling the solar setup, and no one had bothered to steal the panels she'd rightfully stolen in the first place. They were just smashed and scattered.

No one had come in like Goldilocks and eaten our porridge either. Okay we hadn't had any porridge. But we'd had a pretty sizable stash of potato chips, those kettle-cooked ones. Every single bag of those things was "just right," but a bulldozer doesn't give a shit about that. They hadn't slept in our chairs or watched our TV or found Nic's stash of gay porn—or my stash of gay porn—or done anything that any reasonable intruder would have done.

They'd just fucking bulldozed it. All of it. Smoosh. Gone. Goodbye Fort Gaygay (which still needed a better name if you asked me, but Nic thought it was funny, and that girl never thought anything was funny, so I let her have it).

Fort Gaygay would have gone to ruin soon regardless of course. I was off to Evergreen in the Fall, and Nic was . . . she wasn't sure what she was going to do. She'd gotten into every school she'd applied too and turned them all down. She had a ticket to New Zealand and some money saved up, and that was enough for her.

But that wasn't how the end of the fort should have gone. It wasn't right.

"We gotta make them pay for this," I told Nic.

She tossed back her cloak, drew her sword, and held it aloft in the sun. "By this blade, hand-forged by an underpaid craftsman in India and purchased by me at the Oregon Renaissance Faire, I swear we will have our vengeance," she said.

She liked being dramatic.

"Yeah," I said, "we'll fuck them up." I liked being direct.

Neither of us much liked thinking about consequences. But who does?

Even still, can't trash a bunch of bulldozers in broad daylight. We slouched off into the trees, back from whence we'd come.

Nic's parents always let her out at night to see me because they were afraid she'd wind up gay and figured it was good for her to hang out with girls. Which is to say, Nic is trans, but her parents don't know it yet. They still think she's their son. Nic *definitely* is very straight because oh my lord all she ever talks about is boys—she won't shut up—but I guess that's also kind of gay, even though she's a woman. I don't know. Sometimes she calls herself gay, and sometimes she calls herself straight. I just know she only likes boys, which of course doesn't do me any good, but I got over that a long time ago. And around her parents, she calls herself a boy, and at school, she doesn't call herself anything; she just scowls at everyone, and they leave her alone. You think the trench-coat kids are good at scaring the normie kids? Wait till you see the cloak kids. Just the one. Wait till you see Nic.

People take one look at her and assume she has vials of poison under her cloak (she doesn't) or a stash of bizarre homemade weapons in the woods near her house (she does). Mainly though, no one messes with her because even some of the popular kids kind of like her even though they're scared of her. It ain't the nineties anymore. Also, she helps everyone with their homework.

Nic is so complicated!

Not me. I'm a simple girl, born a girl, likes other girls—not Nic, I swear I'm over that. I like chewing bubblegum, and I like listening to bubblegum, and I like Lisa Frank dolphins and shit, ironically but also unironically, and I like vengeance. Like any girl. I call myself James too but only around Nic. Everyone else can call me Jamie. I don't think I'm trans or even really butch or anything. I just like the name James. Who says a femme lesbian can't be tomboy. Or something.

My moms have the opposite feeling about Nic than her parents have about me. See, thing is, my moms are afraid I'll turn out straight, but *I'm* afraid that they're the kind of idiots who call themselves feminists who don't like trans girls. Which isn't fair of me to assume because they've never said anything about it. Maybe they'd be open-minded. Either way. Nic and I haven't told them yet that she's a girl.

They're grateful Nic kept me from failing twelfth grade and eleventh grade and tenth grade, and actually I did okay in ninth grade, but also Nic kept me from failing eighth grade. They just wish I wouldn't spend so much time with her because they don't trust boys.

The important thing is that Nic is able to get permission to meet up with me, but sometimes I have to lie to get out of the house to see her. Especially when my plan was to go see her and then commit an unknown number of felonies that are probably technically ecoterrorism.

So I told my parents I was off to Astronomy Club, and I went out the door and around the block where Nic met me with her dad's beat-up Focus, and we were off to the forest. To what used to be the forest. The clear-cut. We were off to the clear-cut.

When we were younger, we walked there. Walking is for chumps. We had a car now. Sometimes.

"You have tools?" I asked.

She put her finger to her lips and handed me a purse. Shoplifting bag lined with lots of foil between the fabric to keep alarm tags from going off. I opened it, and her phone was inside. I put mine in too.

"Faraday works for cell phones too," she said. "Can't have anyone listening in."

"You gonna line your cloak with tinfoil too?"

"I thought about it," she said, not catching the joke. "But I don't wear it when I go stealing anyway. Too conspicuous."

There was no version of Nic that wasn't conspicuous—with or without a cloak.

"You have tools?" I asked again once the purse was closed and safely in the glove box.

"I have tools," she said.

She didn't elaborate.

All I had was a telescope and some breath mints, so I figured whatever she had was better than that.

"What do you think they're building?" Nic asked.

"Anytime anyone is pointlessly destructive, they're building a golf course," I said. Last year in Social Justice Club, we'd watched a film about the Oka Crisis in Canada when Mohawks had stood down the Canadian Army, defending their land against a fucking golf course. That image had stuck with me longer than Social Justice Club stuck around. A couple of seniors had tried to change our name to the Young Anarchists of America, or YAA!, but the school had vetoed that, and this kid named Beth threw a brick through the principal's office while he was inside of it, and she got expelled, and there went the club. There was some kind of lesson in that story, about the nature of power and the efficacy of various methods of challenging it, but mostly my takeaway was don't get caught.

Which was why we were going to fuck up this golf course at night. With masks on. Like smart girls.

"I bet it's a housing development," Nic said.

"Ooh, maybe a wild-horse slaughterhouse."

"You just want to burn down a wild-horse slaughterhouse."

"What teenaged girl obsessed with Lisa Frank and ponies doesn't want to burn down a wild-horse slaughterhouse?"

"Anyway, they made horse meat illegal to sell in the US."

"They still ship it to Canada."

There was no music behind our bantering. We called it the Diamond Truce. When we were fourteen, we always fought over control of the YouTube, and I played Marina and the Diamonds, and Nic played King Diamond, and we both hated each other's taste, and we finally decided, if we were going to be friends, we couldn't listen to music together.

We parked on a logging road about a quarter mile away from the edge of the clear-cut. Nic pulled out two pairs of thick woolen socks, and we put them on over our shoes to conceal our prints. And we put on ski masks. Which, let me tell you, always makes you feel important. Nic grabbed a duffle bag and threw it over her shoulder, grunting with the effort. I left my telescope on the passenger seat.

Crime always makes you feel like a badass. It's pretty cool. As long as you commit crimes that are okay. Like stealing from chain stores or from your place of employment. My moms got married before it was legal, so they should understand that law and ethics are completely separate topics, but they weren't happy when I tried to explain that to them after I'd gotten caught with a couple hundred dollars in underwear when I was fifteen. Whatever.

Ski masks make you feel badass, but they're also kind of annoying to breathe through. I forgot about that. I hadn't had much cause to wear them in my life.

In the distance, I heard deer barking.

I love the sound of barking deer. I hope I'll never get used to it.

We cut through the woods, avoiding the road, each of us taking a slightly different path, so we didn't leave a trail.

I hadn't liked the look of the clear-cut during the day, but at night, I liked it less.

During the day, it was this . . . field of sticks and stumps, punctuated with huge mounds of even more sticks and presumably some more stumps. Like a giant's field of hay. Not pretty. But growing up in Oregon you get kind of used to them; you can see them just on the edge of the "beauty strips" they leave along the side of the road to try to cover up the damage.

At night, it was . . .

The gibbous moon was almost full (hey I really was in Astronomy Club, but mostly we talked about astrology and annoyed the faculty advisor) and cast pale light on everything. Deep moon shadows made the whole thing high contrast. Honestly, kind of pretty in a macabre, dead-forest-everything-dead-let's-build-a-golf-course way.

The field of death and ruin—I'd expected that. There was something else though.

Nic could sense it too. Her posture changed. She was upright, not crouched in on herself trying to make herself smaller. She was alert.

It was movement, and it wasn't movement. Corner of your eyes only. Some of that might have been the moonlight interrupted by the swaying trees. Some of it might have been night birds or animals. Those deer I'd heard earlier. But some of it? Some of it wasn't.

Walking through that field felt like walking in a dream. The sticks beneath us made our footing treacherous. We weren't using flashlights for obvious, crime-related reasons. Fog sat on the tree line, but everything where we were was clear and pale, almost shimmering, almost glittering.

"A moon-shadowed field," Nic said, "never to cross you, never to know you, for everything you see is not as it should be, and everything you see is as it is."

"What's that?" I asked.

"It's, uh . . . goblin poetry from the *Elsegone Fields* trilogy. The heroes find it in a book right before they're ambushed by talking wolves."

"Cool," I said. "Cool cool cool. Glad I don't believe in that stuff."

Our ruined home—okay, our vacation home—sat at the far edge of the field as did all the heavy equipment. When we made it to the middle of the field, I stopped for a moment to look at the sky.

"The stars are wrong," I told Nic.

"What?" she asked. She looked up but only for a moment.

"They're all wrong. We should be able to see Ursa Major at the very least. And the North Star."

"Well, there's Cygnus," Nic said, pointing to a spot behind us.

"That's not where . . ." I started. But she was right. There it was. The Swan. The Northern Cross. Just . . . not. It was actually too bright, too clear, each star standing out like I was looking at a map that highlighted the constellation.

"It's not right either," I said.

"I don't know what to tell you," Nic said. She didn't like telling me I was wrong, and to be fair, I didn't blame her for that. I don't always respond the best. Nic kept walking.

I didn't really know a ton about astronomy. I was mostly in the club because Anika was the president, and I liked her smile. I must have gotten something wrong.

But . . . who can't find the Big Dipper?

Maybe it was behind the trees.

I didn't like having Cygnus looking down on me, I'll admit. If I'd brought my telescope, I could confirm it really was the Swan by looking for the double star in Albireo at its beak. Even my dinky telescope could do that.

Of course, it was the Swan.

Everything looks wrong by moonlight.

Besides, I had crimes to commit.

I hurried after Nic.

No time to be nervous. Not about the stars, not about consequences.

There were a handful of bulldozers and some . . . I don't know what you call them. *Fern Gully*-style tree-murder machines. And some other machines. They didn't look the same in the moonlight either, though to be fair we hadn't gotten a close look during the day. They were massive. Some were on tank treads, which honestly felt right, like they were machines of war.

We walked past the largest machines and stopped by the bulldozer closest to the remains of Fort Gaygay.

"Alright," Nic said, dropping her tool bag with a heavy clunk. "Let's see what we can do to these things." She pulled out a length of clear hose, I guess to siphon gas.

"No fire," I said, looking over my shoulder, thinking I saw motion.

"Huh?"

"Whatever we do, no fire."

"Why not?"

"Because I'm scared," I said. I didn't say those words very often. "It's too much. What if we catch the whole field or the whole forest? And . . . I think they'll investigate harder for arson." And what I didn't say was that I was afraid someone would see. I was afraid someone was already watching us. Because it felt like someone was.

"Okay," Nic said, hiding her disappointment well, "no fire." She pulled out a large monkey wrench next and a box of sugar.

"Sugar doesn't work," I said. "I read that somewhere. Dirt. Just dirt in the gas tank and the . . . oil tank. I don't know. Add dirt to its insides any way we can."

"Sounds good," Nic said, replacing the sugar. I saw into the bag just then. Another huge wrench. Bolt cutters. A hunting rifle. A medieval mace. Goddam, Nic was weird. "M'lady, will you do the honors?"

I was going to complain about her calling me *m'lady*, but then she dropped to her knees and held out the wrench like offering her sovereign a sword, and I forgave her.

Somewhere at the tree line, close by, something moved. Something big. A deer probably. A really big deer. That sort of looked human.

I was seeing things.

I took the wrench. It may or may not have been necessary to use the wrench to get the gas cap off the bulldozer, but it was a satisfying way to do it nonetheless. Air hissed as the cap came off.

Nic had a mound of dirt held in her cupped hands and was walking toward the tank when we heard a voice.

"Help me!"

It was a scream, a guttural cry. A child's cry. Distant and thin. And echoey. Like through a tin-can telephone. Like from inside the . . .

"Did that just come from the gas tank?" I think Nic said it. Maybe I said it.

"Help me!"

I put my ear to the tank and heard it clearer.

"How the fuck," I said.

"Who the fuck," Nic said.

"What the fuck," I said.

"Help me," the gas tank said.

I looked at Nic, and she dropped the dirt.

"How do we . . ." Nic started to ask.

The shadow came out from the tree line then, and it wasn't a deer. It got bigger, and it walked like a man, but it was taller than a man, and its silhouette was broken and odd like light was coming through, like it was pierced with pins of light, and Nic saw it too, and we met eyes, and I'm pretty sure hers were as full of fear as mine.

"We'll come back for you," I shouted into the gas tank. "I promise."

We ran.

Nic stumbled. I helped her up.

More figures, more giants of starlight, came lumbering from the dark. When they passed into moonlight, they were invisible; then they'd step into shadows and reappear.

We ran and ran, and we didn't stop running until we were at the car, and Nic drove like a madwoman, fueled with fear, blowing through yields and stop signs and red lights, and didn't stop even when we almost T-boned a Subaru, and she didn't stop until we were around the corner from my house, and then she stopped.

She started crying.

She never let me hold her usually. I put my arm around her, and she unbuckled her seatbelt and collapsed against me, and I held her, and she cried and cried.

It was good that she was crying because otherwise I would have had to do it. She was crying for both of us.

"I failed," she said after a while.

"What?"

"I had a rifle. I had a mace. I promised myself . . . I promised myself a long time ago that I'd be noble. That if the world called on me, that I'd answer. Whatever the cost. And I failed."

"You ran from star giants," I said. "That . . . doesn't speak poorly of your character."

"I failed," she said again but softer this time. "There's a kid inside that machine. Right now."

"We'll get them out," I said. "All of them. Being noble doesn't mean being dumb. One rifle versus a dozen creatures that shouldn't exist?"

"Cygnus watch over us," she whispered. "This realm and another, Cygnus watch over us. The Cross, the Swan, she rules every summer sky."

"Is that more goblin poetry?" I asked.

"No," she said. "It's something I saw carved into one of the old science desks at school last year. It's why I know the constellation."

"Well, that's fucking creepy," I said.

"We saw star giants tonight," she offered as a counterpoint. She wasn't crying anymore, but she was still nestled with her head up against my collar. It felt right, having her there. Not that I had a crush on her or anything.

"Fair enough," I said.

"You promised you'd get them out," she said. "Did you mean it?"

"Shit," I said, "I guess I did say that. I guess I have to mean it now."

"Maybe it's safe during the day. They seem like nocturnal things. Tomorrow's Sunday. Maybe no workers either."

"We try again in the morning? Different tools probably. Hacksaw? How the hell do you cut open a gas tank with a kid inside? Can't use an angle grinder."

"I forgot the tools," Nic said. "I forgot my dad's rifle. He's going to kill me when he finds out I took it."

"We'll go first thing in the morning," I said. "Hacksaws. Chisels. Hammers. My mom's got that stuff. We'll figure it out."

"Okay," Nic said. She sat back upright, put her hands on the wheel, and took a deep breath. "Okay. It's gonna be okay." She was talking to herself as much as she was talking to me.

"I wish you could spend the night, to be honest," I said. "I hope that comes across how I mean it." I didn't know how I meant it.

"Yeah," she said. "Me too."

"What a fucking night," I said.

"What a fucking night."

I got out of the car and took my telescope. I was around the corner and almost home before I heard her drive off.

I looked up, and the stars were in the right place. There was the Big Dipper. There was the North Star. There was Cygnus.

I didn't sleep well, which was reasonably predictable. A couple hours maybe. The best (not best) part was the sleep paralysis dream where a swan (okay more like a goose) sat on my chest and stared at me for a brief eternity.

I got up as soon as the first glint of daylight crept through the window. I didn't want to get up. I didn't want to start my day. I didn't want to get dressed, eat breakfast, and walk the couple miles out to the field. I didn't want to face down angry demons or even angry loggers. I didn't want to explain what the rifle in the bag was doing there next to the pipe wrench to anyone who might be there. I didn't want to hear that voice again. I didn't want to keep my promise.

So I just didn't let myself have a choice in the matter, and I got up, and I got dressed. I grabbed some Pop-Tarts: two packs for me, two packs for Nic. I grabbed a bunch of my mom's tools and threw them into my backpack. I went out the door before my parents were even awake. I left a note on the whiteboard. "Off to the woods with Nic. Be back by dinner."

The "be back" part was really the only potential lie.

Arrested girls aren't home by dinner. Dead girls don't come back at all.

Nic was arguing with her mom about something when I walked up, and when she saw me, she turned her back on the conversation and hurried over. "Bye, Mom!" she shouted, and we walked down to the cul-de-sac where the trail started that cut along the creek and then the ravine and then the logging road and then Fort Gaygay—or I guess, a field that somehow both is and isn't in this world.

We tried small talk for a moment, but Nic and I, we've always been more "big subject" kinds of talkers together. That morning, neither of us was trying to broach any big subjects. We dropped the thread soon enough and walked in silence.

We got lucky, if anything could feel like luck just then, and either we beat the crew to work or no one was coming. Who drove those things? Regular humans? Star giants?

We didn't dare walk across the barren field. The sun was out and hot, and it was just too exposed. We circled around instead, through the edge of the forest.

An edge forest is supposed to be dense with undergrowth and brambles and shit. It's like a skin around the muscle of the woods. Walking the edge of a clear-cut is gross and weird because it's like walking through the middle of a forest instead, and it shouldn't be. I couldn't wait for the whole thing to scab over.

There was no sign of celestial beings anywhere.

"We really did see those things, didn't we?" I asked when we were almost to the bulldozers. "The creatures?"

"I don't know," Nic said. "You know me—I want to believe, like the poster my mom has in her office. But I keep running over it in my head, and joint hallucination, mutually reinforced, seems a lot more plausible than . . . than whatever that was."

"But the voice in the bulldozer," I said. "It was so clear."

"I didn't get as good of a listen," Nic said. "I believe you though. Like . . . I believe you as much as I believe myself, or whatever."

"Guess we'll find out either way," I said, stepping out from the forest. The sun felt good on my face, like it always does before it starts feeling not so good. Everything good is like that.

"Guess we will." Nic didn't let the sun touch her face, not if she could help it. Since it was too hot out for a cloak, she had on a wide-brimmed black hat. She thought it made her look like Lydia from *Beetlejuice*, and who was I to tell her she was wrong.

In the daytime, the machines were just bulldozers. And *Fern Gully* forest-murder machines. Just machines. That was obvious. The sun burns up magic like it burns skin, like it fades clothes, like it kills germs.

Nic grabbed the duffel bag, and I went up to the gas tank, which was still open.

"Help me!"

I guess the sun didn't get inside the gas tank to kill that magic.

"Heard it that time," Nic said.

"You keep watch?" I asked. Nic always wanted to keep watch. She's good at posing dramatically, and you need that in someone keeping watch.

"I'll keep watch."

I put a chisel up against the plate steel of the gas tank and swung a hammer.

It takes a really, really long time to disassemble a bulldozer with a chisel.

The sun was high overhead, and Nic was out of water, and I hadn't bothered to bring any, and I was sweating like a madwoman, swinging that hammer like John Henry, and I was pretty sure that, like John Henry, I was (one) going to beat the machine and (two) it was going to be the death of me.

Nic took her turn too but didn't have the endurance for it like I did, so I was the one with chisel and hammer in hand when the gas tank finally fell off, and I was the one with chisel and hammer in hand who finally got a hole in the damn thing.

As soon as I cracked the tank the tiniest bit, two hands broke out from inside like a lizard breaking out of its shell. Those hands ripped the tank open. Having spent the past six hours beating at that thing with a hammer, I had a pretty good idea how tough it was.

A kid climbed out.

Like, a middle schooler.

Wearing a tank top and shorts.

Like any kid in the neighborhood.

Covered in . . . I guessed motor oil by the smell. Not diesel or gas. Motor oil.

"Thanks," he mumbled, looking at his feet. He was shy.

"What the fuck is happening?" I asked Nic.

"A kid just hatched out of the gas tank as a fully formed normie," Nic answered.

"Just checking."

"Hi," I said to the kid who apparently wasn't a figment of my imagination after all. "I'm James. This is Nic."

The kid whirled around, taking in the scene. "Ohmgosh!" the kid yelled.

He ran over to the closest machine, a . . . I don't know what the fuck to call it. Tractor? It had like a scoop on it and wheels. Well, it did at first. This kid ripped through the machine with his bare hands until he reached the gas tank. The tank hit the ground, and another kid ripped it open from the inside.

They each went off to another machine, and you know that whole thing about grains of rice and chessboards? Well, not five minutes after I poked a hole in the first tank, every machine in the field was shredded. Twenty-seven children—I counted twice—ran up to us, singing and smiling and happy and soaked in motor oil.

"Who . . . what . . ."

Before I could formulate my thoughts into a coherent sentence, the sun went out.

I looked up at it. Full eclipse. No corona.

The birds went silent, the bugs went silent, the world went silent. The stars came out.

"Thank you," the first kid said, visibly worried, "but we've got to go. You should too."

They looked thoughtful for a half a moment.

"You could come with if you want," they said to us.

"What?" I asked, struggling to find words. Frankly, I was pretty disassociated. It had taken me a while, but I was getting pretty good at figuring out when I was disassociated. "Where?"

"Into the forest, always the forest," another kid sad, their voice low and sorrowful. "Into the forest to feed on berries, into the forest to fight the machines. Into the forest to flee the giants, into the forest to find the swan."

"First, we'll replant here," the first kid elaborated. "Close the way between these worlds. Keep you safe. All of you safe."

A figure, a silhouette, a star giant, crept into the far edge of the field. It hadn't seen us, not yet. It was walking slow and lazy, confused. Maybe drowsy.

"Just now we have to be gone," a kid said. "You have to be gone."

Now that the light was gone, the children looked different. Straight on, they looked like middle schoolers. From the corner of my eye, they looked like beetles. I mean . . . they were upright. But their skin was glossy and mottled, and their faces went in and out between human features and insectoid. Most notable though, antenna, like horns, sprouted from their heads. Like every devil I'd ever seen in mythology. Worse than any devil I'd ever seen. Like Black Phillip's pet bugs.

"Gone now," the kid said. "Decide. Our home or yours."

"My home," I said.

"Yours," Nic said. She reached out a hand, and a child took it, and they fled toward the woods.

They were gone.

The sun returned.

The giant disappeared.

Nic was gone.

The machines were mangled beyond repair, nearly beyond recognition.

We'd had our revenge.

Nic was gone.

"Where's Nic?" my mom asked when I walked in the door. "I thought you were hanging out with him today."

"She left for her trip early."

"She?"

"She's trans, Mom."

"Oh," my mom said. She thought for a moment. "Well, I hope she has a good trip. I hope she finds what she's looking for."

"Yeah," I said. "Me too."

I had no idea what I'd tell her parents. Or cops if they ever came around. I'd figure that out later. First though, I had a lot of reading to do. Astronomy. Local legend. Cygnus. Cygnus. That fucking swan. Maybe if I found it.

"Can I borrow your car tonight, Mom?" I asked.

"What for?"

"I want to go look at the stars."

{}

Margaret Killjoy is a transfeminine author and editor currently living in a self-built cabin in the Appalachian Mountains. She is the author of the Danielle Cain series of novellas, published by tor.com. The first book, *The Lamb Will Slaughter the Lion*, was released in 2017, and its sequel, *The Barrow Will Send What It May*, came out in April 2018. Her work primarily deals with themes of power and anarchism, as well as gender, social transformation, and people living itinerant or criminal lifestyles. She's also half of the feminist black metal band Feminazgûl and all of the coldwave band Nomadic War Machine. She can be found complaining about things on twitter @magpiekilljoy and on her blog at www.birdsbeforethestorm.net.

BROKEN EYE BOOKS

Sign up for our newsletter at
www.brokeneyebooks.com

Welcome to Broken Eye Books! Our goal is to bring you the weird and funky, the stories you just can't get anywhere else. We want to create books that blend genres and break expectations, stories with fascinating characters and forward-thinking ideas. We want to keep exploring and celebrating the joy of storytelling.

If you want to help us and all the authors and artists involved in our projects, please leave a review for this book! Every single review will help this title get noticed by someone who might not have seen it otherwise.

And stay tuned because we've got more coming . . .

OUR BOOKS

The Hole Behind Midnight, by Clinton J. Boomer
Crooked, by Richard Pett
Scourge of the Realm, by Erik Scott de Bie
Izanami's Choice, by Adam Heine
Pretty Marys All in a Row, by Gwendolyn Kiste
Queen of No Tomorrows, by Matt Maxwell
The Great Faerie Strike, by Spencer Ellsworth
Catfish Lullaby, by A.C. Wise
Busted Synapses, by Erica L. Satifka
Boneset & Feathers, by Gwendolyn Kiste

Stay weird.
Read books.
Repeat.

brokeneyebooks.com
twitter.com/brokeneyebooks
facebook.com/brokeneyebooks
instagram.com/brokeneyebooks
patreon.com/brokeneyebooks

BROKEN
EYE
BOOKS